Beggar

By

H. L. Burke

Cover art by Jennifer White

ISBN-13:
978-1502379900

ISBN-10:
1502379902

To Ash and Evil Twins Everywhere

-Heidi

Chapter One

Leilani Weaver burst out the door of her father's shop and glanced back at her mother. "We'll be late! The launch is in less than an hour."

Her mother stopped in the doorway and adjusted her coat. She wore her "serene" expression. There was no way to rush her once she'd brought her laugh lines into submission and half closed her eyes. That face meant they were going to walk with decorum and dignity, rather than the speed and efficiency Leilani would've preferred. Leilani's sixteen-year-old sister, Keris, glided through the door behind Mother, her chin tilted up and her eyes squinting in an attempt to imitate her. Leilani rolled her eyes. When Leilani and Keris had been eight and ten, Keris was all sorts of fun. Now she spent all her time pretending to be Mother.

Keris cleared her throat. "Ladies don't run."

"And don't worry, Leilani," her mother said. "It's only a twenty minute walk to the water gate." She reached into the pocket of her gray frock coat and pulled out Father's brass pocket watch. "We have plenty of time."

Leilani tried not to grumble. She was too old to sulk or pout, but her mother and sister could be infuriating. Yes, the launch wasn't for an hour. However, if they weren't there early, they'd never get close enough to see anything. Everyone in Gelia City would be attending. Well, everyone except Father and little Kip. Father thought taking time off from work for such things was frivolous, and it had taken hours of begging for Leilani and Keris to get the afternoon off.

Competing as a weaver against the larger shops with their mechanized looms was hard. Father was old-fashioned, though, and liked doing things by hand, with care–another reason the launch of the new steambarge was of no interest to him. "Silly Highmost. They have the Strains at their disposal, but they can't resist puttering around with their clunky machines and noisy contraptions."

Invisible but ever-present, the Strains held the Commonwealth of Gelia together like mortar around the bricks in the city's walls. Nothing moved in the city without their touch. Their use divided the folk of Gelia into two classes. The Highmost could use them with strength, but Common, such as Leilani's family, could coax only small tasks, beggar magic, from the Strains. Common women used them to start fires and to encourage bread to rise, tradesmen to soothe the flaws from the wood and stone they carved, and children to knock fruit and nuts from the highest branches.

Leilani could not remember a time when the Strains did not sing her to sleep at night. They had always been there, like the humming of her father's loom or the smell of her mother's baking or the ticking of their prized grandfather clock.

Her father sang to the Strains as he worked, guiding them to keep his threads from twisting or breaking. Her mother had shown her how to whisper them into submission.

The Strains sounded vibrant and happy today. They revealed themselves in an array of different noises: birdsong, instruments, even human voices. Now, they tinkled like bells, and Leilani's quick steps matched their rhythm. Her high-button shoes tapped against the cobblestone of the narrow streets as she worked her way through the Trade District towards the water gate, one of the three gateways out of the walled city. Here a lock separated the city's six canals, which were built in concentric circles dividing the city districts, from the Seabound

River.

Colorful banners, advertising the wares sold inside, hung from the two- and three-story buildings, built right up against each other. Flower boxes and drying laundry hung over the streets from the upper windows, where most tradesmen and their families lived.

"They say if the barge launch is successful, they might establish a ferry system." Keris's voice sounded distant.

Realizing she had pulled too far ahead, Leilani stopped and waited for her mother and sister.

"My friend, Betta, told me she hopes they'll have a ferry that goes all the way to the sea. I'd like to be able to visit the sea on holidays," Keris continued.

"That seems a long trip, even by steambarge," Mother said.

Ahead, the street opened into a wide courtyard, and Leilani sighed in disappointment. A large crowd, easily a hundred strong, crammed together right up to the edge of the canal.

Leilani could tell the Highmost from the Common by the differences in their clothing. Common wore mainly grays and browns, sturdy work trousers and coats with patches on the arms for the men, long skirts and pinafores for the women. The Highmost dressed in bright colors, and many wore long 'manor robes'–pretentious, ankle-length things–over their clothes. The men wore top hats and tails, and while some of the Highmost women were daring enough to wear bloomer pants and tunics, most sported bustles and ruffled frock coats with pearl buttons. Both kept to tight groups, choosing not to intermingle.

Leilani's cousin Heddie waved from a knot of other textile shop owners and their families. Like all of Leilani's family, she stood out among the fair-haired Gelians. Leilani never feared getting lost in a crowd. Her straight black hair, dark eyes, and small frame kept her from blending in. Both Leilani's paternal and maternal grandparents had immigrated from Rynar, fleeing a famine. As skilled tradesmen, they had been easily assimilated into Gelian culture, though they remained a tiny minority of the population.

"Come on. I've got us a perch," Heddie said as Keris and Mother caught up.

Leilani followed her cousin to a stack of crates. Four small boys already sat on them, but they made room for the older girls. From this vantage point, Leilani gazed over heads and hats to the dark waters of the canal. A flat-bottomed boat, perhaps twenty feet in length, with a waterwheel on the back end bobbed in the water. Four rows of wooden benches sat ready for passengers, though at the moment only a city guard in black leather was onboard.

The Strains changed from bells to drumbeats, a rat-a-tat-tat, similar to falling rain but with a touch more order. Leilani tried to focus on the sound, but the mumbling and murmuring of the crowd beneath her proved too much of a distraction. She sighed. If only she could get close enough to observe how the steambarge worked without so many noisy people in the way. Maybe when the excitement died down, she could ride on it and get a look at the engines.

Heddie squealed, "Oh, look what that lady is wearing!" Leilani groaned, but her cousin kept going. "Silks! Red silks. I wish I had dresses like that. Do you ever wish you were Highmost, Leilani? Imagine what we could wear." Heddie glanced down at her gray, knee-length pinafore and woolen leggings, almost identical to Leilani's, and wrinkled her nose.

Leilani often considered the perks of being born Highmost, and dresses didn't even make the top ten. Hearing the Strains with greater clarity, being able to use them to do fantastic things, having your life devoted to studying their music–those things Leilani longed for. Dresses were just silly.

"You know if you had been born Highmost, you would've been assigned new parents," Leilani pointed out. "You really want that?"

Heddie's grimaced. "Well, Highmost babies are almost never born to Common parents, anyway. Still, it is a nice dream."

"Who in their right mind would dream about that?" Leilani focused once more on the barge.

A Highmost man climbed onto the deck of the steambarge. He dismissed the guard with a wave of his hand, and silence dropped over the crowd like a woolen blanket. Another man joined the first and began shoveling coal into the firebox. Dark puffs of smoke issued from the stack. The water-wheel on the stern cranked to life, and the barge eased away from its mooring. The crowd cheered.

Leilani clapped a few times, so that she wasn't the only one not clapping, then watched. She disliked loud noises, even self-made ones. She preferred just the Strains and her own thoughts.

The Strains whistled over the sound of the applause, loud enough that several people winced. Something about their tone made Leilani scrutinize the scene in front of her. The barge was uneven in the water, the prow sticking out at an odd angle.

Is it supposed to look like that?

The wheel turned faster and faster, and the barge lurched. The man standing at the controls lost his footing and toppled with a mighty splash into the dirty canal.

Leilani's jaw dropped, and her eyes widened in a mix of horror and fascination.

The barge shot down the canal. The remaining crew member dove off. With a crash and a crack, the barge slammed against the wall of the canal and foundered. Steam shot into the air as the furnace sank beneath the water.

The audience gasped and then someone laughed. Soon waves of laughter passed through the crowd, even as someone threw a rope to the waterlogged crewmen. It wasn't every day the Common got to see a Highmost dripping wet.

Leilani leaped from the crates. "Strains, I've never heard

anything that loud. Wasn't that show worth missing a few hours of weaving? Kip's going to be so jealous." She chuckled, imagining what her little brother's face would look like when she told him of the crash.

Her mother shook her head. "Such a waste. Well, it looks as if there will be no launch today. We should get home."

"But, Mother!" Keris exclaimed. "Father gave us the entire afternoon off. Please, may I go for a walk?"

"By that she means she wants to go flirt with the new apprentice at the carpenter's shop down the road." Leilani sniffed.

Keris glared at her. "Jess and I do not flirt. We converse."

"I didn't know conversing involved so much eye-batting." Leilani immediately had to dodge her sister's shove.

"Quiet, you two." Her mother looked down the road towards the house and then back at Keris. "I suppose. And you, Leilani, home or your cousins'?"

Leilani winced. Neither option appealed to her. The Strains hummed, enticing her to go some place quiet and listen. "Maybe I could take a walk along the Farmer's Road? Just until dinner?"

Her mother exhaled a long breath. "I suppose, but please keep your ears open to the Strains. Here." She handed Leilani her satchel. "I packed a few things for us to snack on, but if you're going to be running about in the wild, you might want them."

Leilani grinned, kissed her on the cheek, and darted through the crowd towards the gate.

The Farmer's Road, one of several leading out of Gelia City into the countryside, was pleasantly empty. She ran until the oak trees obscured the city walls behind her.

Away from the bustle of the city with its gas-lamp-lined streets, she could hear the Strains, like a wild symphony, random yet somehow in constant harmony. She imagined weaving them as her father wove his threads.

She veered off the road into a wood. After several attempts resulting in scraped knees, she managed to climb a small tree and hide in the leaves. She played with the Strains, knocking acorns to the ground. She whistled to the Strains, using her voice to guide the arc of the acorns, managing to get some all the way to the rotted-out tree lying at the edge of the clearing.

The Strains warbled a strident call that stood apart from their usual melody. Leilani stopped and tilted her head to the side. She heard a sniffling and mewling followed by a rustling from a nearby thicket. She froze. While she had yet to encounter anything remotely dangerous, she was mindful of the possibility of bears or bandits. She pressed her back into the rough bark of the tree.

A girl, roughly Leilani's age, stumbled out of the bramble. Twigs and leaves stuck out of her downy strawberry-blonde hair. Her reddened, upturned nose dripped. She wore a dirty purple robe and one suede slipper. As she walked, she favored her bare foot.

Seeing the girl's distress, Leilani swung her legs off the branch and braced herself to jump. Before she could leave the safety of the tree, however, the girl gave a frustrated shriek and threw her hands skyward. Following her motion, the Strains tossed the fallen tree several feet into the air. It landed with a cracking of branches in the bracken.

Leilani gaped as the girl sank to her knees, sobbing hysterically. The fear that had risen in Leilani's heart at the girl's outburst died, and Leilani called out, "Are you all right?"

The other child took in a hissing breath and staggered to her feet. Leilani dropped to the ground.

The girl shook her head. "I'm lost."

Leilani nodded. The girl's power and wardrobe meant she had to be Highmost. Highmost lived in the Manor District, not on farms. How had she ended up here?

Leilani cleared her throat. "My name is Leilani. Where did

you come from, and where are you trying to get to?"

The girl smiled and gave a relieved sigh. "I'm Zebedy, but you can call me Zeb. I suppose I am going where I came from, the Country House."

"Do you know where this house is?"

"You leave the city by a gate and go down a road for about an hour by coach," Zebedy answered with an eager nod.

Leilani had little patience for stupidity. She narrowed her eyes and opened her mouth to snap at Zebedy. Before she could speak, however, the Strains chimed, like the tinkling bell that announced when someone entered her father's shop. She paused.

Her mother had told her to listen to the Strains' urgings. *"They are your guardians, given by the Maker, and they can guide you if you let them. They will not lead you astray."*

Leilani tempered her annoyance and spoke softly. "Which gate? The main gate, the trade gate, or the water gate?"

"Oh, well, the one with the blue banners and the statue of the swan."

"The main gate, then." Leilani reached under her cloak for her purse. She opened it and rummaged for her snacks. "Are you hungry?" She offered Zebedy a dried apple.

The Highmost girl took it. "Thank you." She chewed and swallowed. "I haven't eaten since breakfast. I didn't mean to go so far, but the further I walked the louder the Strains grew, and they are so beautiful."

Leilani nodded. "That's why I come here too."

Zebedy's face brightened. "They were telling me all about the trees, about the birds who nest in the tops and the different bugs who hide amongst the leaves. What did they say to you?"

Leilani blushed. "I'm not Highmost. I hear their music but not their words. They really speak to you like that? As if they were people?"

"Oh yes, they say all sorts of things: songs, stories, even jokes. The trainers don't like to admit it, but some Strains can be very funny."

Leilani's mouth quirked in momentary dissatisfaction, but not wanting Zeb to see her jealousy, she forced a weak smile.

Zeb scanned from one end of the clearing to the other. "In the city if I get turned around, I can send the Strains to scout ahead for me, find street signs and the like, but they can only see about twenty feet away from me. Here, in every direction there are trees, trees, trees. All trees look alike, even to the Strains."

Leilani exhaled slowly. "If you came out the main gate, your house is probably to the west."

Zebedy just blinked, so Leilani pointed through the trees.

"That way. I can show you."

The girls walked together in the pale green shadows of the leafy branches. Zeb's tears dried, and she began to babble.

"I'm going to be fourteen in a week. When you're fourteen, the trainers take you on manor tours to see which one suits you best, though you can't join a manor until you're sixteen. I'm a year ahead, so I hope they'll make an exception and let me enroll at fifteen. I want to be with Research. They get to play with pretty much every use of the Strains. The other manors are more restrictive, but I'll take anything, really, except maybe Civics. Civics can be dreadfully dull. One of my classmates at the Country House's mother is Civics, and all she does is paperwork, making sure guards get paid and streets are swept. I'd never be able to stay awake through all that. What do your parents do? Mine are both in the Weather Manor."

"My father's a weaver," Leilani answered, with a shrug. Weaving had never interested her as a topic of conversation.

Zeb frowned, her eyes clouding.

"He's a tradesman."

No reaction, but the frown remained.

"He makes cloth. Sells it to dress shops and tailors or just to the women at market."

"Oh! I bet he knows Marrine, the seamstress at the

Weather Manor. She buys cloth all the time."

"Maybe, but he's not the only weaver in Gelia City, you know. There are at least a dozen weaver shops in the Trade District." Leilani rolled her eyes but forced her face to soften when Zebedy blushed and fell silent. "What do they do at the Weather Manor?" Leilani asked quickly.

"Oh, they predict weather, chart trends, suggest when farmers should plant, and try to intervene if something is going very much awry–to stop catastrophic storms and whatnot. My parents talk about rain a lot." Zebedy laughed and smiled again. Her eyes had cleared, and as the redness faded from her nose, freckles emerged like stars popping into the night sky. She had high, delicate cheekbones and almost invisible eyebrows. Though almost a year younger than Leilani, Zeb stood a good hand taller. Now, Zeb studied Leilani's face.

"You're–" Zeb cleared her throat.

"Rynaran? Yes," Leilani interrupted her, ready to snap if Zeb said anything demeaning. For the most part, Gelians had accepted her people, but they still sometimes said things that made her want to slap them.

"Is it true the Strains don't sing in Rynar?" Zeb asked.

Leilani frowned. "I've never been to Rynar, but my grandmother said she never heard them until their ship landed in Gelia. She thinks the Strains may belong here and here alone, like Gelian wrens or the golden spotted fish which swim in every pond in Rynar but are never seen in Gelia."

Zeb nodded. "I can't imagine living without the Strains."

"Neither can I," Leilani agreed.

The trees thinned as they approached a rutted dirt road. Recognizing it as one of the back roads leading towards the main thoroughfare, Leilani stepped out and glanced up at the skies.

The sun had dropped below the treeline ahead of them. Leilani had told her mother she'd be back in time for dinner. If she turned back now, she might make it, barely. She gave Zeb a sideways glance.

"This will lead to the highway coming from the main gate. Can you find your way from there?"

Zeb opened her mouth, closed it again, and shrugged. "Maybe."

Leilani sighed, loudly. "I hope it's not too far. It will be dark soon."

The two girls pushed on. The shadows lengthened across the road. Zebedy whispered to the Strains, and the air around her hands began to glow, shining pink through her fingers. It made her bones visible and cast a circle of light about them. Entranced, Leilani touched the other girl's hands. She exhaled slowly.

"I didn't even know they could make light. I wish I could do that."

"Here." Zeb took Leilani's left hand about the wrist and hummed.

Leilani's skin tingled and came alight. She smiled.

"Come on." Leilani tugged at Zeb's arm. "Let's get you home."

An owl hooted in the distance, and Zeb flinched. As if in response, Leilani's fingers blinked out. Regret filled her chest. Well, it had been nice to touch something more than beggar magic, if only for a moment.

A twig cracked somewhere nearby. This time Leilani jumped. She pushed Zeb a little harder, trying to concentrate on the Strains and not her own morbid imagination. "We need to walk faster."

Chapter Two

Leilani and Zebedy walked hand in hand. Leilani's legs were leaden and her stomach growled. They had devoured the last of her supplies shortly before sunset, and with the darkness surrounding them and no sign of Zeb's so-called "Country House," Leilani wondered if they would be walking all night.

My parents are going to kill me, if I don't starve to death first. I should've told Zeb I'd take her home with me instead . . . Why didn't I think of that? Too late now. She shook her head and pressed onward.

Cries of animals and the shrieks of night-birds rang through the trees, and shudders traveled down Zebedy's arm into Leilani's.

"Don't worry," Leilani said. "My father told me there's nothing near the city large enough to hunt people."

But with only the faint light from Zeb's spells to guide them, this assurance felt hollow.

"What about people?" Zebedy's voice quavered. "Bad people, Wordless people, bandits and murderers and . . . and *bad* people."

Leilani bit her bottom lip. Her mother had warned her about the Wordless, whose violent acts caused the Strains to no longer sing to them. Crime was rare within the borders of Gelia, for few would risk their communion with the Strains by spilling blood. The worst rumors spoke only of financial evil–trickery and greed–and the Weavers lacked the riches needed to draw such folk to their doors. However, the Wordless did exist, and outside, alone in the night, anything seemed possible.

"We must be almost there," Leilani said.

They walked along the empty highway. Occasionally the woods on either side would open up into great, flat fields or neat rows of fruit trees, but they never sighted a farmhouse. It was too dark to see far from the road. Zebedy swore the Country House would be lit and easily marked, so the girls pressed onward.

After about an hour, voices echoed through the trees, and a smile brightened Zeb's face.

"They're looking for me! They're calling! Come on! We're almost there!" She burst into a run, and Leilani sprinted to keep up.

They turned a bend in the road, and Leilani stared up in bewilderment at the structure before her. Still a fair distance ahead, the red brick house rose like a mountain from behind an iron fence. Lanterns hung from poles on either side of the gate, and the windows within glowed warmly, as if the house watched them with yellow, welcoming eyes.

Shadowy figures with hands glowing like Zeb's trudged through the trees around the house, calling out, "Zebedy! Zebedy!"

"Here!" Zeb cried, raising her luminous fingers to the stars. "Come on. I'm famished."

As they came into the circle of light cast by the lanterns, three adults–a man and woman in their twenties and an older woman with gray hair–rushed to them. All wore draping robes, though the man had his unfastened to reveal a waistcoat and trousers beneath, similar to those Leilani's father wore. The older woman grabbed Zeb by the wrist, her face so stern that for a moment Leilani suspected she would strike the girl. She ran her hands up and down Zeb's arms, whirled her a full circle, then touched Zeb's chin, tilting her head back.

"You seem to be whole," she said. "Blast it, child, where were you? Do you know how many people have been searching for you? And for how long? Have you no sense?"

Zeb, in spite of being years past the age Leilani considered crying appropriate, teared up. Her bottom lip shook.

"I didn't mean to, Mistress Clavia. I just lost track of time.

The Strains were so beautiful in the woods. I won't do it again. I promise!"

The woman's glinting blue eyes softened, and she released the girl. She nodded curtly. "Well, no harm done. Come inside. You must be fed and washed. Another hour and I would've had to send word to your parents. You can thank the Maker it didn't come to that. They might've removed you from my care and then what chance would you have for a good appointment?"

Zeb grinned as she turned back towards Leilani who lingered in the shadows.

"Come on, Leilani. I will show you my room."

"Leilani?" Mistress Clavia's brows furrowed then rose to her hairline when Leilani stepped closer.

Zebedy wrapped her arm about Leilani's shoulders. "This is Leilani. She brought me home. She knows an awful lot about roads and gates and east and west and the like. She can stay with me tonight."

"Miss Zebedy, you can't just pick up stray Common folk. They aren't kittens. I'm sure she has a home and a family she needs to get back to."

Leilani yawned and wavered on her feet. Maybe she would get home after all. "I live in the Trade District."

"That's too far to take her tonight, Mistress," the younger woman said. "Perhaps she can stay in the servants' quarters, and one of them can escort her home tomorrow."

Leilani grimaced. *Well, at least the servants' quarters probably have beds.*

Zeb held Leilani so tight her shoulders scrunched up against her neck. "She's not a servant or a pet; she's my *guest*–and my hero. I never would've found my way home without her."

"That may be, but your parents entrusted me with your care." Mistress Clavia waved her finger.

"My parents say the Maker would have us treat others as we ourselves wish to be treated. It's the foremost command. Is it not?" Zebedy drew herself up like the Sanctified Brothers during Holy Day sermons. "And you said Highmost have a responsibility to the Common, remember? During your Welcome Day speech, you said, 'We have been given greater magic so we may aid those who do not have such powers, not so we may exploit them.' You said that! Well, wouldn't it be exploiting to shove her amongst the servants just because she's Common?"

Leilani swallowed, her eyes widening. Zeb argued with grownups as if she were one. Amongst the folk of the Trade District such impertinence would usually lead to physical consequences.

Mistress Clavia, however, simply exhaled and nodded. "Well, she did escort you home. I will have a cot set out for her. Jonna, take the girls inside and see to it they get some dinner. Parin, make sure everyone knows Miss Brightly has returned, so they can stop searching."

Swept up into the whirlwind of Zebedy, Leilani shut her mouth and enjoyed the benefits. Jonna escorted them up the brick path, through a great, arched doorway, and into a room with a table that stretched on for yards and yards. A white-aproned teenager laid out plates of food at the foot and lit a candelabra. The girls sat, and Leilani picked up her fork. The dish included a breast of chicken, a pile of bright green string beans, and firm but still toothsome lentils.

Zebedy babbled between bites, only finishing about half her meal long after Leilani had scraped the last lentil from her plate. When the servant returned, Zeb relinquished her remaining food. Jonna glided into the room.

"I had your wash basin filled and found a cot and change of clothes for Miss Leilani," she said. "Do you wish me to escort you?"

"No, thank you," Zeb said. "Come, Leilani. I'll show you where we'll be sleeping."

Occasional gas lamps provided a dim, ambient light for the

echoing halls. Leilani stared as they passed into a marbled foyer, under a crystal chandelier, and up a broad staircase. Velvet carpet lined the passage at the top of the steps, and rows of doors flanked either side.

"How many people live here?" Leilani whispered.

"Do you mean staff, trainers, or students?" Zeb asked.

"All, I suppose."

"Well, it varies, then. There are always two trainers per manor–Art, Healing, Civics, Research, Weather, and Industry–and then Mistress Clavia herself, and her assistant, and maybe a dozen servants. I think this year there are a dozen students. Mistress only chooses the ones who show extreme promise. Sometimes she will be in a generous mood come application time and will allow as many as fifty students to enroll, but most years it's under twenty and some years as few as five. Spending a year at the Country House means the manors will fight over you, and most graduates can choose the manor they wish to attend."

"So you divide up into 'manors' the way tradesmen branch off into guilds?" Leilani stifled a yawn with the back of her hand.

"Guilds? I suppose so. Do different guilds specialize in specific things?"

"Yes, my father is a weaver in the textiles guild but there are grocers guilds and carpenters and the like. Mostly, though, it's passed from parent to child. My father is training my brother to take over the family shop someday."

"You have a brother?" Zeb's eyes widened.

"And a sister. My sister, Keris, is two years older and my brother, Kip, five years younger. I was relieved when he was born. My father was set to train me as a weaver. Girls can be tradesmen. It's rare, but if a man doesn't have a son, a daughter works in a pinch. I didn't want to, though."

"What do you want to do, then?"

"If I could pick anything, I think I would be a translator for the Merchant Guild. I speak Rynaran fluently. It's hard to get an apprenticeship in a guild unless you have family connections, however, and my family is made up of craftsmen, not merchants. Merchants get to travel and talk with people from all over the world. I think I'd like that."

"But you might have to leave Gelia . . . and the Strains!" Zeb's voice squeaked.

Leilani shrugged. "Not often, and it's only a dream. Most likely I'll marry another craftsman and learn to help in his shop, like my mother."

Zebedy stopped by a door, identical to the others except for the number "9" carved into the top panel. She put her hand to the latch and pushed it open. Orange firelight surrounded them, and Leilani inhaled the comforting smell of woodsmoke. They stepped inside, and Zeb closed the door behind them.

"This is your room?" Leilani asked. She swallowed uncomfortably. Her entire family shared a living space not much bigger than this over her father's shop. A great bed covered in fluffy looking quilts and four puffy pillows stood against the wall across from the fire. Along the wall opposite the door, a desk rested in the moonlight. Leilani's feet sank into a thick rug. Someone had set up a cot in the middle of the floor, near enough to the fire to be bathed in light, but far enough away to be out of the reach of sparks.

Zeb crossed over and touched the wick of a lantern with her fingertips, setting it alight with the Strains. She replaced the glass shade over the flickering flame and turned up the wick so that the light fell over the desk.

Leilani watched in amazement. It seemed Zeb didn't even need to speak to the Strains to get them to do her bidding. They anticipated her desires. Could they read her thoughts? Was her connection to them that strong? What was it like to be Highmost?

Leilani cast her eyes from one luxury to another, letting out a long breath. Finally her eyes settled on the wooden bookshelf. She knelt in awe before this abundance of volumes and scanned the embossed titles.

"Do these books belong to Mistress Clavia?" she asked, concerned that the Mistress would entrust such treasures to the girl who had lost her shoe in the woods that day.

"Oh, no, all Mistress's books are in the library downstairs. These are just the ones I brought from home, about the Strains mostly, though some are my favorite novels."

"Novels?" Leilani exhaled. Mrs. Weaver had seen to it that all her children could read both Rynaran and Gelian, but books were considered too precious for children. Their family owned two: an ancient tome of Rynaran homeopathic medicine, which had seen their family through many bouts of fever and flu, and the Sanctified Texts, a collection of spiritual works the Sanctified Brothers liked to distribute, even to the poorest families. Leilani had read them both multiple times, though the spines spanned from her little finger to her thumb.

"Yes, novels." Zeb sat beside Leilani with her legs crossed beneath her. She eased one of the thinner volumes off the shelf. "This is my absolute favorite: *The Venture of Sir Marcel*. It has a dragon and a Highmost who sings the dragon into submission and flies him to rescue a princess. There are some 'kissy bits' at the end, but the best parts are all the fighting and flying and magic. Have you read it?"

"No."

"You should. Here, you can borrow it." Zeb held the book out to Leilani who instinctively drew back.

She stared at the red leather cover with fancy golden letters proclaiming the title and author. What did such a book cost?

Zeb's face fell and her freckled nose reddened. "I'm sorry. Do you not like to read?"

"No, it's just . . . if I borrow it, how will I get it back to you?" Leilani dropped her eyes, unwilling to admit that taking responsibility for something as wonderful as that book frightened her.

"I visit my parents once a month in the city. Maybe you can come visit me then." Zeb pushed the novel at her. "Besides, I know the story front to back. I don't suppose I will need to read it again. Maybe when I'm old. Old people can be forgetful, and I would hate to forget how to sing to a dragon with the Strains."

This knowledge, while amusing, didn't strike Leilani as particularly useful, dragons being fictional, but she relented and took the book.

Zeb meandered across the room and sat upon the bed. She gazed at Leilani, opened her mouth, shut it again, then averted her eyes.

Leilani frowned. "What?"

Zeb cleared her throat. "There's a question I like to ask people, but . . . I've never asked a Common person before, and I don't want you to take it the wrong way. I promise I ask *everybody*. Well, everybody I like, anyway."

Leilani narrowed her eyes. "What is it?"

"What do the Strains sound like to you?"

Leilani bit the inside of her bottom lip. "You ask everybody that? It seems kind of personal."

"I just like to know. Everyone I've ever asked hears them a little differently. My parents, for instance, Father says they sound like a man's voice, and they are very stern at times, never musical, but Mother, they talk to her like a child and giggle and sing all the time. Do Common people talk about them?"

Leilani nodded. "Sometimes. We don't hear them alike either. I mean, often they have the same mood, like if the Strains sound happy to me, they probably sound happy to everyone else in the room too."

"I've noticed that! I think they talk to each other."

"They don't have a constant sound to me. I guess that's kind of odd. My other family members talk about whistling or flutes or birdsong even, but it's consistent for them. For me, it changes moment to moment. Sometimes they are instruments, other times voices, never with words, but just sort of humming."

Zeb's face lit up. "That's kind of like me! I mean, most Highmost I've talked to hear only one voice, but I swear I sometimes hear five or six all talking together."

Leilani reached up and pulled a few hairpins out of her bun, freeing her hair. "Have they ever told you what they are?"

Zeb's brow furrowed.

Leilani cleared her throat. "I mean . . . the Sanctified Texts say they are messengers from the Maker, you know, sent to guide and protect us, but sometimes . . . I can always hear the Strains, but sometimes they don't seem to hear me."

Zeb lowered her eyes. "No, they always hear me."

"Forget it." Leilani turned away. What had possessed her to compare her Strains experience with a Highmost? Of course Zeb never felt like the Strains couldn't hear her.

"They don't like to talk about what they are, exactly," Zeb said. "It's frustrating how they dodge questions sometimes, but I can tell when they like people, and they really seem to like you."

Leilani whirled around and eyed the other girl, half thinking Zeb was making fun of her. However, Zeb's eyes looked sincere, apologetic even.

"I didn't mean to . . . I mean, I've never had a Common friend before. We don't have to talk about the Strains anymore, if you don't want to."

"It's fine. I'm tired, though." Leilani rubbed at her eyes, which itched and watered. Her gaze fell longingly onto the cot. The skin of her forehead tightened. It had been an impossible day, in both length and content. The Strains hummed in what could almost be considered a lullaby.

Zeb followed Leilani's eyes. A stack of clothes, neatly folded, sat at the foot of the cot.

"Oh," Zeb said. "It *is* rather late." She stood, walked to a wardrobe, and took out a nightgown. She opened a door hidden in the shadow of the wardrobe, revealing a small room with a washstand and a chamber pot. Steam rose off the water in the china basin. "You can clean up and change. I can't promise these clothes fit, but most of the students are around our age, so they should be functional."

Leilani shut the door to the water closet behind her and awkwardly shed her gray frock, bumping her elbows against the walls. She splashed the warm water all over her face and torso. Then she picked up the cloth hanging from the wall and rubbed her skin briskly until she felt sufficiently dry. She wriggled into the loose tunic and pantaloons provided for her and then emerged. Zebedy slipped into the washroom with her nightgown. Leilani listened to her sloshing and humming for a moment then lay down on the cot and fell immediately into a dreamless sleep.

Chapter Three

The next morning Leilani woke to the sound of Zeb bustling around the room. The young Highmost shuffled, rustled, and bumped. The women in Leilani's family, and even her father to an extent, moved with a cat-like grace, as silent as their shadows. Zeb's stirrings resounded louder than bumbling little Kip.

"Oh, you're up!" Zeb exclaimed as Leilani swung her legs off the side of the cot and stretched her arms over her head. "Good. We can have breakfast together before I attend classes and they escort you home. I'm sure your family has been worried."

Leilani hesitated. In the excitement of the day before, she hadn't stopped to consider how her parents might feel when she didn't return. She had never done anything like this before. All her previous mischief could be classified as word-of-reproof or slap-on-the-wrist-worthy. What would her parents do in response to her disappearing overnight without a word? They might never allow her out of the house again!

"Hopefully they'll understand." She shrugged, imitating her mother's serene face. Did Highmost folk even punish their children? Zeb seemed to do pretty much whatever she wanted without consequences. Leilani envied her freedom.

Zeb wore a crisp tunic and bloomers, identical to the ones that had been provided for Leilani, except better fitting. She slipped her purple robe off a hook by the door. It couldn't have been the same one she wore the day before–that had been hopelessly torn and dirtied–but a similar garment with yellow thread embroidered about the cuffs and collar.

Zeb whispered, "Come on, do me up."

The Strains sang as the bronze buttons along the front of

her garment slid into place, closing it almost to her chin. Zeb smiled. Leilani raised her eyebrows. Her mother had always taught her to use the Strains sparingly, never for simple tasks one could do with one's own hands, lest they tire of such drudgery and refuse to work when Leilani needed them to. Zeb showed no such reservations. Leilani supposed such was the natural result of being able to hear the jokes the Strains told her.

"I've been thinking about when we can visit," Zeb said. "I won't be able to get to Gelia City for several weeks, and students aren't supposed to have visitors. It distracts from our studies. The good news is, you will have more than enough time to finish that book."

The novel Zeb had thrust upon Leilani the night before lay under the cot. She had fully intended to "forget" it. Now, however, Zeb fetched it and handed it to Leilani.

Leilani's clothes sat in a heap at the foot of the cot. She picked up her frock. Other than a few patches of lingering road dust, the garments were wearable. She brushed them off and donned them before following Zeb down to the dining hall.

The curtains along the wall were drawn back, revealing a row of tall windows. In the daylight the furnishings held less of a mystique though they kept their grandiosity. In fact, now that the sun revealed the vines carved into the backs of the chairs and reflected on the waxy shine of the table top, Leilani felt even more impressed and out of place. Her mother washed their sturdy, oaken furniture daily and sanded it twice a year, but even with all the scouring, it never shone.

About half the seats held children, ranging from twelve to maybe sixteen. All wore robes identical to Zeb's. Their plates had different portions of pancakes and bacon remaining. Some children scraped the syrup off their empty plates with their utensils while others still picked at their first few bites.

Two chairs stood empty before two waiting plates. Zeb grabbed Leilani's arm and held her back. The young Highmost wrinkled her nose.

"They put us across from Vickers. He's so obtuse."

Leilani glanced at the boy who seemed to be a few years older than her. He had dark eyes, brown hair, and skin more tan than the typical Gelian. Most tended to be fair and freckled like Zeb, but Vickers looked as if he spent a lot of time out in the sun without burning. At their approach, he grinned. Zeb stuck up her nose and glided into her seat, pulling Leilani along.

He swallowed. "I hear you got lost, Whistles."

"Whistles?" Leilani furrowed her brows.

"That's the sound the wind makes blowing through her empty head."

Zeb sniffed. "My empty head has trounced your rock-filled one on multiple occasions."

"Only because you never stop talking. If you say enough, eventually you'll say something right, if only by accident. My mom always said, 'you let loose enough chickens in the garden, and they'll eat all the bugs, just gobble down your vegetables while they're at it.'"

"That makes no sense."

"You make no sense."

"Ha ha, clever. You must be an expert on all things poultry. No wonder you're so fowl."

Vickers rolled his eyes and took another oversized bite.

Leilani sensed that their bickering was more habitual than angry, so she concentrated on her breakfast.

Zeb turned back to Leilani. "Hopefully, I can convince my parents to let me have a few hours for our visits. They get possessive of me on holidays," she said, nibbling on a piece of bacon.

Vickers snickered. "They probably want to make sure you don't wander off. Maybe they should buy you a leash."

"I'm sorry. I don't understand clucking," Zeb retorted.

Leilani laughed, and Vickers shot her a glare. Not one to be intimidated, even by an older boy, Leilani narrowed her eyes at him.

He tilted his head. "Be careful about tagging along with Whistles here. She's planning to enter Research Manor. She might want to experiment on you."

Zeb's face reddened. "Don't be ridiculous."

Vickers kept his eyes on Leilani. "It's true, though. Research does all sorts of twisted experiments, sometimes even on people. They like to find . . . unconventional ways to use the Strains, and sometimes that can go very, very badly." He glanced at Zeb and smirked when she glared at him.

Leilani snorted. "The Strains wouldn't hurt anyone. They aren't weapons."

"The Strains won't *kill* anyone. There's a lot you can do to a person without killing them. My father is with Healing Manor. He's told me horror stories of what people can do with concentrated Strains: cuts, bruises, broken bones . . . even blindness."

A shudder ran down Leilani's spine. He had to be lying. The Strains wouldn't hurt people. They couldn't.

"You're just being nasty. Research doesn't experiment on *people.*" Zeb stabbed her fork at him.

Vickers shrugged, holding up his butter knife to block her. "Maybe not any more, but you know the history as well as I do. It's happened."

"Decades ago, and all that is illegal now. You're just trying to scare her. Don't listen to him, Leilani."

"I thought I should warn her. Whether she's smart enough to listen isn't my problem." Vickers took a large bite of pancake.

"Sweet of you to worry about me, but I'll take my chances." Leilani rolled her eyes. She knew boys like him. Her older cousins used to try to frighten her with scary stories about monsters in the cellars. She wasn't going to let Vickers get a rise out of her that way.

A bell rang and students pushed back chairs and brushed crumbs from their robes. Vickers laid his flatware in an X across his plate and smiled. "We'll have to continue this scintillating discussion later. So long, Whistles. I'll beat you at the debate tonight. Oh, sorry. I meant *see* you." He stood.

"Good-bye, Vicky," Leilani said, forcing her mouth to remain in a straight line, though she wanted to smirk at him. He winced but strode away without another word.

Zeb chuckled. "Vicky! I'll have to remember that."

Miss Jonna approached the girls, and Zebedy sighed.

"You have the book?" she asked.

Leilani held it up and nodded. "Thank you. I can't wait to read it."

"I really want to see you again. My parents always take me to the Botanical Gardens on holidays. Perhaps we can meet there? It's open to the public, and I'm sure your parents wouldn't mind."

"It's time for your friend to go, Miss Zebedy. The wagon is waiting for her," Jonna said gently.

Zeb's shoulders slumped. She then pulled Leilani forward into a bear hug. Leilani raised her eyebrows and patted the other girl's back.

"I'll send word to you when I'm back in Gelia City," Zeb said. "Good-bye, Leilani."

"Good-bye, Zeb." Leilani followed Jonna out of the room into the courtyard where a wagon waited. She was sad to leave Zeb, the Country House, and her first real adventure behind.

§

Leilani shuddered as the wagon turned onto Loom Lane, the street in the Trade District that held her father's shop. The ride from the Country House had seemed to stretch on forever, though from the level of her hunger she surmised it to be only mid-morning.

Her heart sank to her toes even as the Strains chimed in time with the horse's hooves on the cobblestones.

The doors of every shop beckoned in foot traffic. Colorful banners fluttered above each entry way, naming their specialty, be it the weaving of fine silks or rough canvas. All except one. The door to her father's store stood barred shut, and his flag had not been unfurled. Her father *never* closed the shop. Well, except on Holy Days and for festivals, but all shops closed for such occasions.

"Stop here!" she squeaked at the man who drove the wagon.

The middle aged servant raised an eyebrow but pulled rein.

Leilani swallowed but couldn't moisten her arid throat. She gripped Zebedy's book against her chest and exhaled slowly through her nose, the way her mother did when trying not to scream at young Kip.

"Is this your home, Miss?" the driver asked.

She nodded.

"Do you want me to come in with you?"

She shook her head. Whatever the consequences, she would own up to it. She wouldn't cry. She would be calm and collected like her mother, dignified, as suited the daughter of a skilled Rynaran craftsman.

She slid from the wagon seat and thanked the driver. He smiled and waited until she had turned away to shake the reins and urge the horses onward.

The city, even on a quiet street such as Loom Lane, was never silent. People roamed down the length of the cobbled road, which was swept clean daily by the apprentices of the nearby shops. She could hear murmured conversations slipping through open doors. She listened to the Strains. They hummed somberly, a mix between cooing doves and the low twang of her mother's Ryanaran fiddle.

"We are Gelian now," her mother often said. "We belong to this city, and we prosper as she prospers. However, we must never forget the dignity of our forefathers and what they left behind in Rynar where the Strains never sing."

Leilani reminded herself, *Gelians are expressive and bold.*

Rynarans are calm and pragmatic. I am both. I will be bold but calm. I did what I had to do and my parents ***will*** *understand. I will make them understand, as Zebedy did with Mistress Clavia when she pleaded last night.*

A boisterous Strain rose above the rest, trilling like a bird, and she wished with all her heart she could hear the lyrics to its song.

The Strains joked with Zebedy. Perhaps they would reassure Leilani now.

She whispered to them, a wordless hiss of melody. True beggar magic rarely employed words. The Strains shaped around her song, harmonizing with it. Coaxed by the music, they grew in strength and followed her to her father's door.

She pushed at the door and found it was not bolted. The bell rang at her entry, and she stared at the counter stacked with samples of cloth and the great, upright loom beyond, one of many her father owned and worked at. Footsteps clattered down the stairs and her big sister swept into the room.

"Leilani! Where have you been? Mother and Father have been out searching for you since daybreak. I think they even contacted the guard. All of Gelia City must be looking for you." Keris threw her arms into the air. As calm as she pretended to be, Keris loved the dramatic, so Leilani could hope she exaggerated. Still, she had been gone a long while.

Eight year old Kip wandered in from the other room.

"Stay here with Kip. I will try and find someone who knows where they are. Oh, you are in so much trouble, little sister." Keris clicked her tongue with obvious relish but ruffled Leilani's dark hair affectionately as she brushed past her and out the door.

Leilani sighed.

"Hi," Kip said. "I thought you might've died. Keris said if you weren't dead you would be when Dad got his hands on you."

Leilani's stomach clenched.

Kip glanced around the shop. "I'm hungry. Keris's porridge is slimy. Will you make me some cake? Or can I at least have an apple?"

Glad for the distraction, Leilani accompanied her brother into the cool cellar beneath the shop where her parents kept their provisions. She wouldn't risk further angering her parents by breaking into the precious sugar, but an apple or two would not be missed. She reached into the barrel and pulled out two red cheeked apples. Kip snatched one and crunched a large bite, reminding her of Vickers.

"What's that?" He reached his sticky fingers towards the book.

Leilani drew back protectively. "Don't talk with your mouth full."

Leaving him in the cellar, she hurried up the ladder and then the stairs into the loft where her family slept. Each of the Weaver children owned a small chest for their treasures and holiday clothes. She tucked the book under her silken slippers and shut the lid.

Kip wandered upstairs after her and sat, spinning a painted top on the wooden floor. Leilani thanked the Maker he didn't want to talk.

The door bell chimed again, and Leilani's heart faltered.

"Please, Maker, let them understand. Make them listen," she prayed.

"Leilani!" her mother's anxious voice called out.

Her mother met her halfway up the stairs with a fierce hug, then withdrew, gripped her shoulders tight, and gave her a quick shake.

"Child! Where were you? What were you thinking? Why . . ." She trailed off and pulled Leilani back against her chest.

Leilani squeezed her eyes shut. She had been in no real danger, but knowing how she had frightened her mother shamed her.

"I'm so sorry," she wept. "Oh, Mama, forgive me. I didn't mean to."

Mrs. Weaver released her daughter and wiped her own eyes with the back of her hand. "Well, you're all right. You must be hungry. I will make you lunch, and you will tell me where you were last night, and then we shall decide what to do about it. Keris went to fetch your father. He's searching along the Farmer's Road. I want to know *everything* by the time they return."

Leilani followed her mother through the workroom into the tiny kitchen. Her mother ruled over this space like a queen at court. She could make feasts from the scraps of the previous meal in moments and spent hours on Festival Days creating masterpieces that filled bellies and delighted tongues. Their house often hosted big meals for uncles, cousins, aunts, and any neighbors who might be less blessed in relations than the Weavers.

The brick fireplace, painted white and swept clean, took up an entire wall of the room. On the opposite wall, a small window nestled in the midst of shelves and cabinets filled with the tools of Mother's art: mortar and pestle, sieves, pans, pots, china, apothecary jars containing precious spices, and mesh bags of dried vegetables. The space smelled of smoke and onions.

Her mother opened a cabinet and took out a loaf of crusty brown bread and a wheel of cheese: typical Gelian fare, hearty and simple. Leilani's mother could cook both cuisines artfully, but Leilani admitted she preferred the bold, salty taste of Gelian cheeses to the more subtle Rynaran flavors where the main course tended to be well cooked rice and steamed vegetables.

Her mother took a long knife and cut into the loaf. Leilani's mouth watered, but she dutifully told of her encounter with Zebedy and what had come of it. She even mentioned the book for fear that an omission would be as bad as a lie.

Mrs. Weaver nodded and set the slice of bread, now

spread with soft white cheese, in front of her daughter. "You did well. You could not leave the girl alone and lost. The Maker would approve of your kindness and His laws are greater than mine. I'm not sure your father will see it the same, but I will speak with him."

Leilani's father held tighter to Rynaran tradition where unquestioning obedience to a parent or king was a high virtue. He spoke with pride of how, as a child, he had burned his hand rather than tell his mother that the pot she had asked him to carry was too hot. Still, even he laughed more than he scolded, and Leilani did not fear him.

Relief settled over her, and she picked up the bread and began to eat.

Her mother continued to bustle about between the table and the cabinets. She fed the fire and sorted bottles. Her brows furrowed as if these tasks took a good deal of concentration.

Leilani finished the meal and stood to take her plate to the washing bucket.

"Leilani, my child," her mother said.

Leilani turned to her.

"You will not be disappointed if this girl neglects to contact you." From her mother's tone, this could've been either a question or an order.

Leilani swallowed. "Why wouldn't she?" After all, Zeb liked her. They even talked about the Strains. No one had ever talked with Leilani about the Strains like that before. Surely you didn't share such things with someone only to abandon them. That wouldn't be right.

Her mother took the plate from her and washed it carefully in the bucket.

"No laws say the Highmost must not converse with the Common, but we are chickens in the barnyard and they are doves in the garden. Our lives are filled with work. The Highmost? Who knows what they do in their great manors? There is a gap between our worlds, Leilani, and she will most likely forget you."

"But she gave me her book." Leilani's throat constricted.

"Little one, such things are trifles to the Highmost. This Zebedy can afford many books."

Leilani's lunch sat heavy in her stomach. She lowered her eyes and nodded. She didn't want to believe what her mother said, but what if she was right? What if Leilani was nothing at all to Zeb?

Her mother touched her shoulder. "Perhaps I am wrong. Perhaps your Zebedy is wise enough to see your value as a friend, but try not to hope. Read your book, treasure your memories, and be satisfied."

Chapter Four

Two weeks after Leilani's adventure in the woods, the letter arrived. Unlike most of the Weavers' mail–which they fetched once a month from the Messenger Guild in the Merchant District–it came to the door. The apprentice who brought it, a boy of perhaps fifteen, pulled himself up and presented the letter to Mrs. Weaver as if he were an ambassador delivering a grand treaty. Mrs. Weaver thanked him and offered him a cookie. He accepted it, blushed, and mumbled in an artificially low voice, "Thank you, ma'am."

"Mother, what does it say?" Keris clasped her hands in front of her chest. "Oh! Is that a wax seal? In red? So official, perhaps it is an invitation . . . to a ball."

"Yes, and you'll leave your sandal behind and marry the Rynaran emperor's son like in grandma's stories." Leilani rolled her eyes. She forced her feet to stay planted on the floor and not dance about. She had her own hopes as to what might be in the envelope but dared not voice them.

Her mother slid her fingernail around the seal until it gave and the envelope popped open. The children inhaled as one.

"Well," Mother said. "Leilani, this is for you."

Leilani's hands shook as she took the precious document. Her father came away from his loom and leaned over the counter to watch. Four sets of eyes bored into her as she read aloud.

"Miss Zebedy Brightly requests the honor of Miss Leilani Weaver's presence on the 5th day of High Spring at midday in the Botanical Gardens. Lunch will be provided."

"Oh, it *is* an invitation!" Keris squealed. "And she called you *Miss* Leilani, like a little grown up."

Leilani wrinkled her nose at Keris then turned her hopeful

eyes towards her mother. "The fifth is tomorrow. May I go?"

"The Botanical Gardens are all the way in the Leisure District, and Father and I have work to do," her mother said.

"You let Keris go with Jess to the last festival in the Merchant District. The Leisure District isn't that much farther," Leilani pointed out.

Mother sighed. "Well, the guards keep the streets safe. Tray, what do you think?"

"Well . . ." her father drew out the syllable as he walked around the counter. He smiled and wiped his hands on his pant legs. "It's all right with me. Soon enough we'll have to do without both of our girls, after all."

Leilani stood still, holding her precious letter. What would it be like to spend an afternoon among the Highmost? Would she be expected to behave prim and proper like the stories Grandma used to tell where girls balanced pots on their heads to learn to walk like perfect ladies? Oh, and the book! Leilani had read it three times over and had hoped to read it again, but Zeb would want it back.

Of course, none of that mattered. Zeb had kept her promise!

That night Leilani stared into the darkness with the book clutched to her chest. She wondered what the day would bring. What would Zeb's parents think of her? Would she look out of place in her Common clothes? At least she knew they wouldn't have better table manners, not if Vickers was any indication of the average Highmost.

Finally, about mid-morning, when Mother could no longer find chores to busy her, Leilani hurried out the door.

The Trade District made up the outer ring of Gelia City's five circles. To get to the Leisure District, Leilani would have to pass through the Merchant District, filled with markets, banks, and money changers, then Civics Circle where the guards who watched the cities roads trained and the Highmost-appointed-judges held court.

Leilani had never been beyond the Leisure District, but she knew that the center circle, the Manor District, housed the homes and workplaces of the Highmost.

The bridges over the canals were staggered about the rings–her father said to make it harder for would-be invaders–so when Leilani crossed one she had to go at least a quarter way around the circle to get to the next. Every so often she would pass a pair of guards, clad in black leather doublets with silver metal cuffs on their wrists.

At last she reached the wide, white stone bridge spanning the water way between the Civic Circle and the Leisure District. Before her rose the gleaming spires of the Cathedral, three in total, each higher than the one preceding it. A golden flame crowned the tallest, brilliant in the mid-day sun.

There was so much more sky here than in the cramped streets of the Trade District and so much green that for moment Leilani thought she had stepped out of the city and back into the woods. While the main road continued up to the Cathedral, dozens of little paths led off through the manicured trees.

Signposts at the head of each path indicated attractions such as "Aviary," "Heroes' Monument," and "Amphitheater." Leilani sighted one labeled "Botanical Gardens" about half way up the road. She started to run, but heard her mother's voice in her head, "Do you want to be so out of breath you can't even say 'hello' when you find your friend? Walk like a lady."

Like a quick lady, Leilani decided. She kept her steps fast but her manner composed.

She traveled down the path through speckled sunlight, passing benches and fountains and folk picnicking on the grass. A rose covered trellis made a gateway in a tall, green hedge. She walked through this into an open green field. Leilani stopped short.

Grids of waist-high hedges divided the field into segments, each of which appeared to be a complete garden in its own right. Sculpted topiaries filled one area and roses another. A great hedge maze with walls taller than a grown man beckoned from behind a fountain and a lily pad covered duck pond.

Leilani strained her neck this way and that in search of Zebedy.

"Leilani!"

She whirled around and found Zebedy running down the path towards her.

"You're right on time of course." The younger but taller girl tackle-hugged Leilani then looked back over her shoulder at a couple strolling hand and hand. "My parents can be so slow sometimes. I feared you would tire of waiting and go home before we got here."

Leilani smiled. "Never."

The Brightlys approached. Leilani drew herself up, hoping to make a good impression. Zeb seemed to accept her even though she wasn't Highmost, but would her parents?

Both of the Brightlys had graying, light brown hair and crow's feet around their eyes. They wore identical sky blue robes.

"So this is the young lady who saved our little genius." The man chuckled, his kind smile putting her at ease.

"My name is Leilani."

"Zebedy mentioned that you had aspirations towards joining the Merchant Guild," Mr. Brightly said as he led their small group down the gravel path to the maze.

Leilani blushed. "They are just dreams, sir."

"Ah, but dreams are admirable things. Never dismiss a dream. I mention it now because you might be interested in the greenhouses. The merchants are our best source of exotic plants. They bring back many fine specimens from their trips abroad."

"I want to show her the maze, Father," Zebedy said.

"In good time, Zebedy. You may be on recess, but one should never stop learning. The greenhouses are most educational."

They detoured onto a path that went around the perimeter of the maze rather than through it. On the other side stood a long glass house with a rounded roof, like half a transparent pipe, but so full of leaves that the glass appeared to be green at first glance.

"Open up," Mr. Brightly said.

The door swung open. Leilani swallowed. She had forgotten how casually the Highmost used the Strains.

They stepped inside and another word from Zeb's father set the door back in place. Warm, humid air wrapped around Leilani like a blanket as smells straight out of her mother's spice jars wafted to her nose. Along with those odors came floral scents, intoxicating and calming. She swayed. The Strains whistled a low, flute-like melody.

Zeb grabbed her arm. "Oh no. He's here."

Leilani glanced around. "Huh? Who?"

Zeb pointed forward.

The plants crowding the space before them left only a narrow walkway covered in dried moss. Leilani squinted through the fan shaped leaves and hanging flowers and saw a bench at the end, up against the far wall. On it sat a young man, reading.

"Can we go to the maze now, please?" Zeb asked.

"We just got here," Mrs. Brightly answered. "I think this is the new fern species from Ollare. Research and Healing have been fighting over samples for months now." The adults admired a feathery, blue-green plant.

Zeb fidgeted, glancing from the boy on the bench to the exit. The rangy young man looked up, tucked his book under his arm, and rose. Zebedy stepped behind her father. As the youth unfolded to his full height and the sunlight hit his dark hair, Leilani recognized him.

"Oh, Vickers," she said.

Zebedy nodded, her mouth puckering.

Zeb's classmate ambled towards them. He stood a hand

taller than Mr. Brightly, his size belying his youthful face. Leilani hadn't noticed that the first time she met him.

"Hello, Zebedy," he said.

Zebedy stepped out to face him. "Hi."

Leilani stood at her friend's side, ready to defend her should Vickers prove hostile.

"Zebedy, dear, is this a friend of yours?" Mrs. Brightly asked.

"Just a classmate."

Mrs. Brightly raised her eyebrows, and Zeb sighed.

"Mother, Father, this is Vickers Buffet. Vickers, these are my parents, and you've met Leilani."

"Buffet? You must be Rigel Buffet's son then. Are you fifteen?"

"No, ma'am. Nearly seventeen, actually."

Mrs. Brightly nodded. "You are a junior fellow, then?"

He shifted from one foot to another. "No. Unfortunately, my desired manor had a hiring freeze due to budgetary issues. Rather than settle for my second choice, I arranged to stay at the Country House another year."

"Budgetary issues." Mr. Brightly raised his palms to the sky as if nothing more needed to be said. "Do you intend to go into the Healing Manor like your father? The Buffet name is quite the legacy to live up to."

"No, sir. I start my fellowship at Civics this winter. I have a head for statistics and figures. My, uh, people skills are less developed, and I've been told my bedside manner would never allow me to be a sympathetic healer."

"Well, you seem quite well spoken to me." Mrs. Brightly beamed. "I'm glad Zebedy has such accomplished and promising classmates."

Vickers's dark eyes stared at Zeb. "Your daughter is quite talented in her own right."

"Thank you," Zeb said but averted her gaze from his.

He nodded. "I have studying to do. I will leave you folks to your outing."

Zeb's eyes stayed on Vickers as he walked past them and out the door.

"What a nice young man. We really should have more of Zeb's classmates over for tea." Mrs. Brightly turned back towards the intriguing fern.

"Mother, please, can we go to the maze now?" Zebedy begged.

Mrs. Brightly sighed. "I suppose. Go have fun. Your father and I wish to see more of the greenhouses."

The girls hurried away. Once outside, Zebedy looked around. "Whew, he didn't linger. It's infuriating how he can pretend to be such a gentleman with grown ups around, as if he actually had a soul."

"You *really* don't like him. Is it because he's going into Civics? You said you didn't care for Civics."

"No, it isn't that. It's a long story, but Vicky is my *nemesis*."

Leilani mulled over this as the girls took the path back to the maze entrance. She had never known anyone with a nemesis before.

Zeb took her hand when they stepped into the maze. She grinned. "The idea is to get as lost as possible. It raises the stakes when you have to find your way out. Come on!"

Hand in hand the girls ran down the shadowy paths, making random turn after random turn. Finally they hit a dead end and sank to the packed earth, out of breath and laughing. Zeb glanced over at Leilani who looked down and saw that she still held the book in her hands.

"Oh, you brought that. I'd almost forgotten," Zeb said.

Leilani passed it to Zeb.

"Did you like it?" Zeb asked. "Oh, of course you did! How could you not? Which was your favorite part?"

"When he first tames the dragon and they go flying together over the forests and into the mountains, riding among the whistling Strains." Leilani leaned back against the hedge.

"Oh, I like that bit. Though the battle between the two dragons towards the end is better, just in my opinion."

They sat in silence for a moment before Leilani cleared her throat. "For a nemesis, Vicky is awfully nice to your parents."

"He's sneaky that way. When we first met, I thought we would be great friends. Then I realized what a complete blackguard he is."

"What did he do?"

Zeb's face reddened. She exhaled slowly. "He's older than me, you know, and when I first got to the Country House he had already been there for two years. Madame Clavia considered him her star student. His father has been in the Highmost Seat several times so everyone expects Vickers to have an amazing future in whatever field he chooses."

"Highmost Seat?"

"Oh, I forgot you wouldn't know about that. It's hard to explain. The Seat is an elected position among the manors. No one can hold it for more than five years at a time, so it switches frequently, but whoever holds the Seat settles disputes between the manors and things like that."

"Ah, like when the guilds meet and appoint a Chairman for the year."

"Now I know nothing about that, but sure, sounds about right. Rigel Buffet has held the position four times, which is some sort of record. Every time he's been eligible to run, he's won.

"Anyway, my first night at the Country House, I felt really homesick, so I wandered into the library. Vickers was there, alone, reading. He reads a lot, better with books than people, which generally I admire, books are wonderful, but . . ." Her eyes clouded, and she ground her palm into the dirt. "Anyway, we started to talk, and because I was lonely, I told him all about myself. He seemed like such a good listener. He didn't talk much except for one story he told me about his mother. It was so funny, about her chasing chickens around the yard and finally giving up only to have one land on her head when she sat sulking."

Leilani laughed, but something in Zeb's eyes made her smile fade.

"So how did he get from there to being your nemesis?" she asked.

"Well, the next evening all the students were gathered for one of Madame Clavia's discussion sessions. She likes to pick a topic and just have students gab about it, throwing back and forth ideas and observations. Coincidentally, the topic that night turned out to be flight, whether men would ever find the means to fly and how birds managed it. Vickers had the floor for most of it. I know I mock him, but he's highly intelligent, which is actually part of the difficulty with him. If he were stupid he would be dismissible, but anyway, he lectured for a bit about avian aerodynamics, and I decided to make a joke referencing his story. I forget exactly what I said, something like he should know all about birds since his mother was a chicken expert. Everyone just stared at me.

"There are stares and there are stares, you know. These stares were as if I'd just said something terrible. Madame Clavia got all serious and said, 'Now, Miss Zebedy, that was cruel.' I remember her words exactly, even if I've forgotten my own. I think after a bit she saw how confused I was because she took me aside. She explained that not only was Vickers's mother an important senior fellow at Healing Manor, not someone who would ever be chasing chickens around, but that she had been dead a little over a year, and it isn't kind to make fun of dead parents."

Leilani furrowed her brow. "So the whole story he told was a lie?"

"Apparently. I was so humiliated. It's one thing to have people think you are stupid or careless, but to be labeled as cruel? That I couldn't bear. Anyway, no one would talk to me for a long time. Vickers tried once, but he wouldn't admit to lying, so I shut my door in his face. I realized he probably intended for me to make a fool of myself. He told that lie knowing I'd repeat it and look silly."

"That's horrible. Do the other students still not speak to you?"

Zeb grinned. "Oh, they speak to me all right. I took my revenge with style. Along with the discussions, Madame Clavia sets up formal debates once a month. She gives out the topic and team assignments a week in advance and, like with everything, Vickers was considered the reigning champion.

"Anyway, I spent every spare moment in the library, researching and plotting and when debate day came, I claimed the floor. You should've seen his face when I defeated him. Those big brown eyes of his looked like a stunned puppy dog's. I almost forgave him for a moment, just because of that." She laughed. "So, anyway, since then we've been academic rivals. You know, as much as I loathe him personally, when he leaves the Country House, I will miss the challenge he provides."

Leilani nodded. Zeb's world sounded so interesting. Kids living in their own spaces, no chores, reading . . . on the other hand Zeb appeared to spend more time away from her family than with them. Leilani wouldn't like that at all.

"Common have guilds rather than manors, right?" Zeb asked. "They sound similar."

"Yes, well, there are individual trades within guilds. My father is part of the Textiles Guild which includes other weavers but also tailors, thread spinners, and even basket and rope makers."

"Rope makers? Somehow I can't imagine sitting around all day making rope. Basket weaving might be fun, though. I think I could use the Strains for that." Zeb raised her hands in an exaggerated shrug. She stood and brushed off her bloomers. "Come, let's try and find our way out, and no consulting the Strains. That would be cheating."

Leilani scrambled to her feet. "No Strains." She didn't

mention that she didn't have the ability to use them as guides in the first place.

The girls spent the day darting through the hedge maze, climbing trees, and talking. Zeb's parents checked on them from time to time but seemed to trust their daughter to take care of herself. After a few hours, they wandered to the far side of the Gardens where vendors had set up colorful tents and sold everything from sweet cakes to whole, roasted chickens. The savory smells tickled Leilani's nose. Her mouth watered. Zeb had pocket money, and the two friends split a flat cake crusted in sugar and a whole fish skewered on a stick with the head still attached and black grill marks on its scales.

Zeb fell silent as they ate.

Maybe she's lost her voice, Leilani thought between bites of fish.

Zeb cleared her throat.

Leilani glanced at her and swallowed her mouthful.

"That day with Vickers, I asked him to be my best friend, because I'd never had one before. He said yes, but then he didn't really mean it. I haven't tried to have a best friend since then, or really any friend for that matter." Zeb dropped her eyes. "I mean, people like me, but mostly adults. Other kids . . . they don't like to talk about the Strains like I do . . . or you do."

Leilani took a handkerchief from her pocket and cleaned the fish oil from her fingers. The Strains chirped the way they had the day in the woods when she'd first met Zeb.

"I've never had a best friend either, until now." She smiled at Zeb.

Zeb's face glowed.

Chapter Five

A few days after her visit with Zeb, a letter arrived for Leilani. She snatched it up and read it over and over again.

Zeb wrote about Vickers's impending departure and how everyone at the Country House acted as if he were leaving for war rather than accepting an overdue manor posting.

I'm pretty sure his head has grown several inches in circumference, but he won't let me measure. I do regret that he's leaving. No one else presents a suitable challenge or makes decent conversation. I wish you could come take Vickers's place. Maybe you could teach me Rynaran.

Zeb had enclosed enough postage for Leilani to write back. She stayed up late composing a perfect letter.

Keris's boyfriend has been around a lot. His name is Jess. He's a carpenter, so he has no business looking at cloth so often. Everyone knows he's just here to drool over Keris. She likes it. It's ridiculous.

She only wants to talk about him now, so I really wish I were there with you. I bet I could teach you Rynaran. Keris knows it but says it isn't fashionable. By that she means Jess doesn't speak it.

She finished off her letter with some examples of Rynaran shorthand, along with their Gelian equivalents, including both her and Zeb's names.

As the weather grew colder, they moved their meetings from the Botanical Gardens to Weather Manor, where Zeb's family lived. Zeb's Country House schedule allowed her three days at home a month. Although she spent most of this time with her parents, she always managed to visit with Leilani for a few hours.

Weather Manor, a grand, brick building, had communal

recreation rooms where Highmost families socialized and ate together. Most didn't give Leilani a second look, but a few times a squinting adult approached her and asked if she were lost. After that she made sure to stick next to Zeb. Those at the manor seemed to know Zeb and didn't question her peculiar taste in company.

Keris continued to meet with Jess, and as weeks turned to months, it seemed as if the young man became a member of the family. Even Father, who mumbled at first about Jess being "too Gelian," grew to like the affable fellow. No one was surprised when, after six months, he asked for Keris's hand.

Zeb gaped a bit when Leilani told her. They were meeting, once again in the garden as the winter had finally thawed away. The air still had a bite of cold to it, which stung Leilani's lungs.

"But she's only a little older than you. Sixteen, I thought," Zeb said as they strolled down a shaded path.

Leilani shrugged. "Seventeen. We both had birthdays months ago."

Zeb frowned. "You should've told me. I didn't get you a present. I would've gotten you a nice one. I'm good at picking out gifts."

"I don't need presents. Birthdays aren't a big deal." Leilani pulled her cloak closer about herself, even though she wasn't that cold.

A present from Zeb would have been nice. It might've been a book, even, but what could I give her back? A yard of cloth? She shook her head. It was best to avoid the exchange of gifts.

"Anyway, sixteen or seventeen, that seems awfully young to get married," Zeb continued.

"Not really. My parents were both seventeen when their parents arranged their match, and my grandparents were even younger. If I don't find a trade that suits me by the time I'm seventeen, they'll most likely consult the matchmaker for me."

Zeb stopped before a wooden bench, brushed a few stray leaves from the seat, and sat down. "But you will find a trade, won't you? You're still going to apply for the Merchant Guild."

"Father won't let me until I'm closer to sixteen, so I have at least six months. I've been practicing my Rynaran. They need translators." Leilani eased herself next to her friend. She didn't mention that the surest way to get an appointment within the Merchant Guild would be to marry a merchant. That seemed like such a mercenary reason to choose a spouse, and Leilani didn't want to consider it. Keris had suggested that Leilani should dress up in her best and go flirt with the merchant apprentices. Leilani shrugged off the suggestion and told her sister that love had turned her into an idiot. Leilani hoped she wouldn't lose her ability to think if she ever fell in love.

"I know you'll get it. They'd be foolish not to accept you. Maybe you can even work with the merchants who collaborate with Industry Manor. Then we can work near each other."

The wind rustled the leaves around them and the Strains twittered, blending in with the birdsong.

"They sound happy today," Leilani said. "Playful even."

"They like the spring. They're always checking in on the way things grow. That's why my mother chose weather. She loves how the Strains respond to the sun and the rain and the wind. I love it too." Zeb shifted on the bench. "You know, my father has connections in Industry Manor. I bet he can get you a recommendation. We should go talk to him right now!"

Leilani raised her eyebrows. "Right now?"

Zeb bounced off the bench and started down the path, not waiting for Leilani to agree.

Leilani sighed and followed after.

Weather Manor was made up of sturdy, red brick structures covered with vines and filled with bubbling fountains. The buildings almost looked natural, as if they'd been grown rather than built.

Zeb led Leilani into the office sections. A large wooden door separated the work spaces from the public lobby. In front of this sat a heavy wooden desk with a stern looking older woman behind.

"That's just Parrie. I call her the 'gatekeeper', but she's more of a secretary," Zeb whispered as the two girls approached. "She looks a lot meaner than she is. She's supposed to keep people from bothering my parents and their co-workers during office hours, but she always lets me through."

Parrie narrowed her eyes at them, and Leilani swallowed.

"Miss Zebedy, you know people are working here. Your parents are very busy." Parrie raised a finger.

"I just need to talk to my father for a moment. He doesn't mind," Zeb assured her.

Parrie frowned.

"Please?" Zeb clutched her hands in front of her in a praying position.

A smile weakened the corners of Parrie's mouth. "All right, but go straight to his office and then straight back. No poking around with the meteorological equipment again."

Zeb took Leilani's hand and pulled her towards the doors.

Parrie bolted up. "No, just you. This . . . young lady is not a member of the manors."

Leilani's face burned.

Zeb scowled. "Leilani is my friend, and Father doesn't mind."

"She doesn't belong in here. The only *non-manor* folk allowed in the work areas are servants and aides. She can wait for you out here." Parrie pointed to a bench across the empty lobby.

"No, she–"

"Zeb," Leilani interrupted. "It's fine. You'll only be a minute. Let's not make a fuss."

"But it isn't fair." Zeb glared at Parrie.

"It's how things are. If you'd rather, we can wait until he's off and talk to him then."

Zeb exhaled a loud breath. "All right. I'll be right back.

Don't think this means I agree with you, Parrie."

Parrie shrugged and opened the doors. She then smiled a simpering smile at Leilani. "It is good to see a respectful young lady who knows her place in the world."

"I don't know my place," Leilani said. "But I know plenty about people like you."

Parrie's face contorted, but Leilani spun on her heels and went to sit on the bench. The Strains twanged in a way that almost resembled laughter. She smiled with satisfaction. Parrie glowered for a bit then returned to reading over some paperwork.

Leilani stared at the marble floors. There was some sort of pattern in the blue and gray tiles, either waves or wind. She traced them around the empty room.

Minutes ticked on and she got up and paced. Parrie kept her eyes on the documents, occasionally making notes with a fountain pen.

Leilani walked to the far side of the room where several high windows let in squares of light. She stood with her face to the sun and imagined herself as a merchant's apprentice, translating important documents from Gelian to Rynaran.

The Strains began a song, a dashing, dancing fiddle tune. Leilani couldn't help swaying along with it. She closed her eyes as the music built to a crescendo.

Then, for no discernible reason, the music grew weaker; not weaker as in softer, but more distant, as if the fiddler walked away from her, then faded altogether.

It felt as if cotton was stuck in her ears. Why couldn't she hear them? She cleared her throat, just to see if she'd lost her hearing altogether, and the sound echoed in the emptiness. Whirling around, she spied Parrie.

Parrie still continued with her paper work as if nothing had happened. What if it was just Leilani who couldn't hear the Strains? Where were they?

"Come back," she whispered, praying they would answer

her.

Nothing.

Dead silence.

She was alone.

Overwhelmed, Leilani stumbled backwards two steps, and the Strains swelled to meet her like welcoming friends. She breathed a sigh of relief. "Where were you?" she chided.

The fiddle music commenced but in a somber key. Leilani rubbed her arms, trying to calm the goose-bumps which prickled all over her skin. She concentrated on the sounds.

Don't leave me again. I couldn't bear it.

The door behind Parrie flung open, and Zeb darted across the lobby, waving a piece of paper in her hand.

"I've got it! He wrote it out the moment I asked."

"Shhh!" Parrie hissed.

Zeb wrinkled her nose. "I told him you wouldn't let Leilani in. He said that wasn't very professional of you."

Parrie's jaw dropped, then she hardened her face and harrumphed.

Zeb hurried to Leilani's side and handed her the letter. Leilani gazed down at it, somehow unable to smile.

Zeb's eyebrows furrowed. "Are you all right? Parrie wasn't nasty to you while I was gone, was she?"

"No, it's not that. I'm just . . ." Leilani paused.

What was that? I've never not heard them, not even for a second. What could that mean? Nothing. Of course, nothing. They had to have been there. They were simply quiet.

"I'm just tired," she said. The Strains continued to harmonize, and she convinced herself all was right. Still, doubt chewed at her. What if they left again?

"Oh, all right. Let's go someplace where we can sit down then." Zeb cast a disapproving look over her shoulder at Parrie. "Some place with better company."

Chapter Six

Mr. Weaver touched Leilani's shoulder. "I'm sorry, but you knew this was a likely outcome. The Merchant Guild only takes on so many apprentices, and they like to keep things within their families."

"I just thought my language skills and Mr. Brightly's recommendation would give me a leg up," Leilani mumbled.

Her father took the letter out of his daughter's hand and placed it on the counter, as if removing it made any difference.

She had been waiting for this letter for a month, since a week after her sixteenth birthday, the earliest her father would allow her to apply to the guild. Every day for weeks either she or Kip made the trip to the messenger's guild to check for a response. Today had been Kip's turn, and he brought back the letter, only to have it be a refusal.

The only dream Leilani had ever possessed, the only dream she dared to imagine, had died. She had carefully chosen a practical dream and not set lofty, unattainable goals. Probabilities were calculated, skills honed to improve her chances, and she convinced herself that this really could happen.

And now that they said no, now what?

"You don't need to seek a trade," Kip said. "You can stay here and help me when I take over the shop."

Leilani winced. *Great, I can be my baby brother's apprentice. That's a lofty fate.*

"He's right, Leilani," Father said. "You will always be welcome here. However, I know you must wish to leave the nest. Perhaps one of the other shopkeepers in our guild has need of an apprentice, or we could consult the matchmaker on your behalf."

Leilani hesitated. None of the trades within the Textiles Guild interested her, but they appealed to her more than an arranged marriage, especially since she had seen how happy Keris was, ruling over the little home her love had produced. Leilani wasn't in love, however; no puppy-eyed young man had presented himself to her the way Jess had tripped over his own feet to win Keris.

There had to be a better option. In spite of the finality of the refusal, she glanced at the letter. Perhaps if she read it again, it would say something different.

Mrs. Weaver cleared her throat. “It isn’t as if you have to settle in an apprenticeship this very minute. Your visit with Miss Zebedy is tomorrow. Why don’t you go upstairs and ready your festival dress? You can’t go to the manors in your work frock.”

Grateful to escape her family’s sympathy, Leilani slumped up the stairs. She took her gown out of the chest and shook it off. No wrinkles.

In defiance of her mother’s dire predictions, Leilani’s monthly visits with the young Highmost had continued. In fact, since Zeb had turned fifteen and graduated the Country House, they saw each other more often. Preparing for her first manor post took up some of Zeb’s days, but she had returned to live with her parents in the meantime. The girls saw each other two to three times a week. Zeb even visited the Weavers' home on occasion.

Zeb’s academic career had charted a skyward course, due to her quick wit and sensitivity to the Strains. Of all the Highmost Leilani had observed, none related to the Strains like Zebedy. Most treated the Strains as a servant or a tool. Zeb named them, laughed with them, and interacted with the musical voices as one might a beloved older sibling.

Sometimes when Leilani and Zeb conversed, the Strains joined in. Leilani could hear their music and guess their mood, but Zeb would giggle at their jokes and relate clever observations they made. Even among the Highmost, Zeb was special.

Zeb would be a much welcomed distraction. Leilani wouldn't even tell her about the Merchant Guild's rejection. For the space of their visit, it would be as if the letter had never arrived.

§

Weather Manor housed both the homes and work spaces of the Highmost assigned to it. Each building spanned an area as large as the Textiles District and from the outside appeared to be one gigantic structure. The majority of the housing had been built into the thick outer wall, and balconies dripped with potted plants and colorful flags displaying family crests.

Through the gate, however, lay a labyrinth of passages and buildings more complex than the Botanical Garden's maze. Tunnels led under houses into courtyards. Ivy walls lined pathways from homes to offices to shared recreation areas where Zeb had taught Leilani to play Toss Stone and card games.

Leilani took the stairs up to the Brightlys' third story apartment two steps at a time. She tugged at the bell rope, and the door burst open.

Zeb grinned. In her hand she clutched a piece of parchment similar to the one that bore Leilani's ill news. For a moment Leilani's smile faded. The Strains whistled with an up-note she almost imagined to be a question. She forced a smile.

"You're here! Come in! I have so much to talk about." Zeb took her hand and pulled her through the sitting room into the bedroom.

Though Leilani had only seen the inside of the Brightlys' home, Zeb had informed her that all the Highmost quarters shared the same two bedroom and a sitting area layout. Their meals came from the shared kitchen with its army of cooks and porters. Even their baths were communal, a luxurious, heated affair where people often socialized.

"What if a family has more children?" Leilani had asked,

having noted that Highmost, even at the Country House, rarely shared bedrooms.

"We just don't . . . have more children, that is. I've never thought to ask why."

Leilani didn't press the issue. Her mother always cautioned her about meddling in personal matters.

Zeb's artwork, watercolors filled with vibrant shades and swirling shapes which represented the Strains, decked her walls. Three bookshelves overflowed with volumes, many of which Zeb had loaned her over the last year. Purple curtains matched the coverlet of her bed and the dozen or so pillows. The plush carpets were starry sky blue. A mobile of silver stars twirled from the ceiling. Leilani loved Zeb's room.

Zeb sat on the bed, then stood and glanced out the window only to jump on her bed three times before collapsing cross legged into the cushions. No longer required to wear her Country House uniform, Zeb wore simple tunics and pantaloons in various colors, periwinkle today.

She laid the folded parchment before her. "Oh, I wrinkled it. Would you fix that for me?"

The Strains hummed like Mrs. Weaver when she busied herself in the kitchen, wielding her wooden spoon like an artist's brush. The creases in Zeb's document flattened and vanished.

"Thank you. I want to keep it forever." Zeb sighed and looked up at Leilani with sparkling eyes.

"What's the letter?" Leilani asked.

"My future!" Zeb unfolded it and held it forth.

The paper bore a lot of letters in fancy, near indecipherable calligraphy. Zeb took it back before Leilani got further than, "To the honorable Miss Zebedy Brightly, graduate of Madame Clavia's Academy for the Gifted . . ."

"You're supposed to query all the manors, to see where there are openings, in case your first choice doesn't want you. Well, I only want Research, but Mother said Research is the most competitive manor, and she made me send out multiple letters, one to each manor, even Civics." Zeb's nose wrinkled. "Anyway, letters went out and letters came back. Accepted Weather. Accepted Healing. Accepted Art, but no news from Research until this morning." She waved her paper in the air.

Leilani laughed. "Congratulations."

Zeb sprang off the bed and twirled around, waving the letter so fast the flapping page sounded like a bird taking off. Leilani stared at her exuberant friend, and her mouth twitched. The disappointment of her own rejection returned full force, but she forced her face to remain impassive. Zeb was happy now. Leilani couldn't ruin that. The Strains droned in a minor key.

Zeb stopped mid-spin and faced Leilani. Her lips quirked downward, and her brows came together. "The Strains say you are sad. Why are you sad?"

Leilani shook her head. "It is nothing."

"No, Leilani, you don't get sad over nothing. People call you names, you snap back. A dog could bite you, and you'd bite back, but you don't get sad. If you are sad–and the Strains say you are, so don't lie–there must be a reason."

Leilani cleared her throat, shuffled her feet, and murmured, "The Merchant Guild said no."

"But why?" Zeb dropped her precious letter and pulled Leilani into an awkward hug. Zeb's chin poked her in the forehead. Still, Leilani preferred that to looking Zeb in the eye.

When Zeb released her, Leilani concentrated on the carpet.

"What will you do?" Zeb asked as she stooped down to retrieve her letter.

Leilani shrugged. "There are other guilds, other trades. I don't have to decide right away."

Zeb nodded, folded and unfolded the letter, and sat back down on the edge of her bed. "Leilani, there is . . . well . . . I assumed you would get your apprenticeship, but perhaps your misfortune is my fortune. Do you know about manor fellowships?"

"Aye, that's what you applied for, isn't it? It's like an apprenticeship but to a Highmost manor rather than a trade."

"Sort of. Since I've been accepted into Research Manor, I will live there now. I will also be assigned an aide."

Leilani frowned and said nothing.

"An aide is an assistant of sorts. They have to be clever because they see to a fellow's–that's what I am now, a fellow–anyway, they see to a fellow's schedule, help them write papers, do research, all sorts of tasks.

"It's an important job. Usually the aide is Highmost, but they don't have to be. Anyway, there is no law. I checked a long time ago in case you changed your mind about the Merchant Guild. Father knows people in Civics–they're the manor that oversees assignments."

Leilani swallowed. "Are you asking me to be your aide?"

"Yes! I can't imagine working with anyone else. Think how much fun we could have? In our own apartment? I have so many ideas for projects. Of course, for the first years of my fellowship, I'll be assisting a senior fellow, but either way, so much fun!"

Leilani chewed her bottom lip. She loved Zeb like family, like a boisterous, exhausting little sister. Still, Zeb could be overwhelming. Did Leilani really want that every day from now on?

"I don't know, Zeb," she said. "Wouldn't you essentially be my boss? Wouldn't that be awkward?"

"It's me, Leilani. When have I ever been bossy?"

"Do you want an exact number? Do you have a counting frame?"

Zeb frowned at her. "I'm not that bad. You always have a choice."

"'It's easier to ride the current than to fight the tide,'" Leilani used one of her grandmother's favorite expressions.

Zeb stuck out her bottom lip, but in the same moment her face brightened. "Yes, but it has always been a fun ride."

Leilani laughed. "Yes."

"You don't have to, I guess, but . . . if you don't, once my fellowship starts, we'll never see each other. Junior fellows rarely leave the manor. My mother always told me once you were in an apprenticeship and I in a fellowship, there simply wouldn't be time for us to be friends. I swore I wouldn't let that happen. You're my best friend, Leilani."

Leilani avoided Zeb's pleading eyes, trying to think logically about the matter. The Strains tickled her ears, a tinkling noise this time, like thousands of miniature bells.

Zeb grinned. "The Strains think you should."

Leilani sniffed. "So you say."

Zeb shook her head until her hair covered her face then brushed it behind her ears. "I would never lie about the Strains. They'd throw a fit if I did."

The bells hit a crescendo, perhaps the loudest Leilani had ever heard them. Zeb's smile nearly squeezed her eyes shut.

Leilani had envied Zeb's place at the Country House. This could be her chance, her only chance, to experience the Highmost world. Would she fit in? After all, she was Common, and as much as Zeb tried to sell it, an aide sounded a lot like a servant.

The Strains grew louder, until the ringing almost became unbearable. If they wanted it so badly, it had to be for a reason.

Leilani smiled. "All right, Zeb. Sounds like a plan."

Chapter Seven

Leilani tried not to gawk as she followed Zeb through new sections of the Manor District, but there was so much to look at. She'd only spent time at Weather before and had expected the other manors to look the same. Each manor, however, had a particular aesthetic. Civics Manor stood cold and stately with the lived-in sections hidden behind a facade of pillars and sweeping stairs.

Art Manor opened up to the air with tall, stained glass windows back-lit by skylights so the colors shone outward. As she and Zeb passed it, she stopped to stare. Three abstract marble sculptures stood on the brick pathway leading up to the open gate. Each resembled sea spray, cast up into the air then twisted into a form that was almost human but not quite.

"What are those supposed to be?" she asked.

"They're called, 'the Emergence of Creativity,'" Zeb answered.

Leilani blinked at her.

Zeb shrugged. "I don't understand it either, but Art fellows like things that don't make sense."

The Strains whistled, and Zeb grabbed Leilani's hand. "Come on. We're almost there."

Research stood between Art and Healing. Unlike the other manors, which at least pretended to be one large edifice, this manor looked as jumbled as the block cities Leilani had made with firewood scraps as a child. A dozen or so smaller structures of varying heights surrounded a rounded building with a domed roof. A long cylinder, as big as a tree and tipped with a glistening lens jutted from the cupola.

"That's a telescope. The whole Observatory deck can turn to look at different celestial bodies." Zeb's eyes shone. "Look there." She pointed to a towering structure with a scaffolding exoskeleton. "They're rebuilding again. Research is always changing to accommodate new projects. We'll be in the main building, under the Observatory. That's where all the apartments and most of the offices are."

They joined a short line of about twenty young people, most dressed similarly to Zeb, though a few still wore their colored robes, indicating which school they had graduated from. Zeb nodded to a blonde girl in purple.

"Marce Regale," she murmured. "Of course the show off is still wearing her robes. Regales are all about who they know, not what they can do. I bet her daddy got her the appointment. The trick with her is to be polite but guarded or else she'll step on you on the way up the ladder. You should've seen her flirt with Vicky."

"Maybe they deserve each other," Leilani said.

Zeb's cheeks flushed. "I haven't seen him in a year. Maybe he's matured. Either way, he was always too smart to buy into Marce's act."

The Observatory's tall double doors opened, and the group filed forward. Leilani glanced down at her gray frock. Zeb had said they would assign her a uniform so there would be no point in wearing her best clothes. Maybe these folk were all fellows, not aides, but certainly none of them were Common.

Leilani's heart quailed. Had this been a mistake?

Inside they found themselves in a vaulted hallway with checkerboard marble floors and dozens of bust-filled alcoves. A tall woman with short cropped hair wearing a frock coat and bustled skirt, all in severe black, waved them over.

"Welcome, junior fellows. I am Mistress Straight and for the next six months, I shall be overseeing your health and well-being," she said in a calm, cool voice. "Do not be deceived. I am not your friend, and if you cannot abide by the rules or handle your workload, I will be happy to show you the door. However, I am your protector. If you feel you are being treated unfairly or if you do not have the tools you need to thrive, I will give you a fair ear. Junior fellows are students, not servants, and you deserve respect and dignity."

Twenty-two heads nodded, even Leilani's though she knew the speech did not apply to her.

"Some of you have requested specific aides. The rest of you will have your aides assigned, and they will join you tonight after supper. Now, for your current assignments."

Mistress Straight snapped her fingers, and a young man in Common clothes stepped from an alcove. He carried a tall stack of papers.

"I want to assure you all that we at Research take extreme care in assigning junior fellows to their senior fellow mentors. The decision takes into account your aptitudes, academic history, and even your personalities as determined by your exit interviews with previous teachers.

"When my aide calls your name, step forward and receive your packet. On it will be detailed your senior fellow assignment, as well as your room number, maps, and other information you will require in your first days at Research. Once you have this, you may proceed to your individual apartments to freshen up. Your belongings should have been delivered ahead of you. You will be expected in the dining hall promptly at six. A bell will sound indicating ten minutes' warning. Directions to the dining hall are provided in your packet. Now, Revi, please read the names."

The Common man stepped forward and cleared his throat. "Vasily Able."

A young woman came forward. The aide bowed and handed her the paper. She looked it over, nodded, and continued down the passageway.

"Zebedy Brightly."

"Come on," Zeb said.

Leilani followed her friend as she claimed her documents. Zeb took off after the last girl with determined strides.

"Vye Devotes," the aide continued calling out names.

"I've toured this manor three times," Zeb said. "The junior fellows' quarters are this way."

Zebedy walked briskly, her head held high.

Ahead the hallway met with another, and in the transecting space sat a circular bench underneath a chandelier. A young man in a dark leather uniform with silver bracers strode in a slow orbit about this, shifting his eyes from one passage to another. He had curly brown hair and alert gray eyes. His face had a boyish softness, and though a guard, he couldn't be much older than her. He caught Leilani's gaze and smiled. She blushed, embarrassed to be caught staring.

An older guard marched up the hall from the right. The younger turned to face him, sheathing his blade. Leilani watched in bewilderment as the men's fingers flashed through various strange motions. The older man pointed down the way he'd came, then to the younger man, then tilted his head to the side with his hand against his cheek. The younger man nodded, saluted, and left his post. His replacement began his circuit as Leilani and Zeb passed.

"What was that, with their hands?" Leilani asked.

Zeb shrugged. "Many manor guards are deaf. That's how they talk. Some of it you can guess the meaning of, if you try."

Leilani's brows furrowed. "Deaf?"

"Yes." Zeb nodded. "Father says it makes sense because the Strains can leave you if you have to kill, even in the line of duty. Occasionally the guards have to use force, and Civics found years ago that guards were skittish when it came to risking the loss of the Strains to stop a robbery or quell a riot. Fortunately, that sort of thing doesn't happen very often nowadays, but anyway, they still like to hire guards with little to no attachment to the Strains."

"I've met guards before, and I don't think any of them were deaf," Leilani said. "I've never even heard of a deaf guard."

"It's a manor thing." Zeb shrugged. "Even in the manors it

is only a small percentage of the guards."

Leilani glanced at the retreating figure of the young guard. Silence, forever silence, no voices, no music, no Strains. And yet the guard's eyes had sparkled. What would it be like to never hear the Strains? Her thinking slowed her pace, and Zeb outdistanced her.

Zeb glanced back. "Catch up, Leilani." She stepped forward, and her entire frame crumpled. Her shoulders slumped, her legs gave out, and she sat down with a whimper. Half rolling, half crawling, she scrambled back towards Leilani. Her eyes widened.

"What is it?" Leilani asked. "You didn't forget to eat breakfast again, did you? Are you going to pass out?" She knelt next to her friend and touched her forehead. She didn't feel cold or sweaty.

Zeb pulled herself up, closed her eyes, and breathed. "Please be there, please . . ." She exhaled and opened her eyes. "I couldn't hear them for a moment. They're back now."

"Them? The Strains?"

Zeb's head bobbed up and down. "I have never not heard them."

Leilani offered her friend a hand up. Zebedy clung to her. Together they edged forward with small, hesitant steps. Zeb paused after each and tilted her head this way and that. Leilani listened. The Strains hummed in their quiet, ever present way. They did seem subdued today. Perhaps that was what Zeb meant.

Then the girls stepped into absolute silence. Zeb's fingers sank into Leilani's arm. Leilani's jaw dropped.

Sometimes the Strains were subtle, like the hiss of sand slipping through an hourglass. They would fade into the background and wait to be called. They could be overlooked and ignored, but they were never silent.

Except that day at Weather Manor.

Leilani had almost forgotten that horrible experience, but

there had been a moment, a split second without the Strains. Now the silence endured, and it wasn't just Leilani who noticed. Zeb felt it too.

Zeb's whole body trembled. Chills shot up and down Leilani's spine. No Strains. She whistled, waiting for them to harmonize. Nothing.

"Please come back," Zeb whispered. Her face had grown pale. Afraid her friend was about to swoon, Leilani pushed her onward. A few steps and the music swelled to meet them. Zeb closed her eyes, and the color returned to her cheeks.

Leilani released her friend and returned to the void, the dead spot. The air felt thin. Closing her eyes, she could almost imagine herself in a tomb, trapped with the dead. She forced her eyes open, rubbing her suddenly goose-bump covered arms. She hopped in and out and walked through. The first time it measured three paces across, the second two, the third one, and the fourth time she couldn't find it at all.

Leilani bit her bottom lip. "What was that?"

"I don't know, but I don't want to stay here." Zeb took off at a run, down to the end of the hall and up a short staircase. A series of doors awaited. Zeb matched the number, 32, on her paper to the door, and pushed her way in. "Should we tell someone?" She sat on one of the two twin beds and drew her knees against her chest.

"Tell them what? That for a moment we couldn't hear the Strains? We can't show them where. The dead spot only lasted for a minute."

Zeb frowned. "It isn't natural. I don't like it."

Chapter Eight

The next day Zebedy wouldn't talk about the dead spot.

"Today needs to be a dream," she said when Leilani brought it up. "I don't have time for nightmares."

Leilani's aide uniform consisted of a red tunic with a high collar and black leggings. Zeb had gifted her with a leather messenger bag filled with "tools of the trade" and helped her put her hair up in a bun with copper pins. Leilani tried to return the favor by braiding Zeb's hair, but the strands were already escaping from the ribbon to fly about her friend's face.

Leilani assumed there would be some housekeeping involved, but Zeb informed her there was a staff specifically assigned to cleaning and the like.

"Don't worry. If you need to do something, I'll let you know. For now, just keep me company. We meet Fellow Brash right after breakfast."

Zeb gushed about her assigned mentor, Fellow Brash, during their communal table breakfast. "He's young for a senior fellow. Last year his team oversaw the installment of sensors around the manor ring to measure the strength, volume, and variety of the Strains."

"Perhaps he'd know something about the dead . . ." Leilani began, but Zeb's eyes stopped her. For a moment the blood drained from the young Highmost's face, and Leilani feared she would collapse again.

The girls finished their meals in silence, Zeb picking at her porridge. The serving staff cleared the girls' plates away, and Zeb rose.

"Brash's workshop is in one of the exterior buildings." She avoided Leilani's questioning gaze. The girls started down the hall. They passed a small, iron gateway held in place by an inch-wide silver ring. Leilani stopped. Behind it descended a dark stairway.

"What's in there?" she asked, not used to seeing barred doors in Highmost areas. Between the guards and the Strains, locks were unneeded.

"Oh, that's a Strains-proof lock. I've never seen one before." Zeb touched the ring and rotated it to reveal a tiny keyhole. "Normal locks can be picked using the Strains, so most people don't bother with them. This is silver. Imbued silver if I'm not mistaken. Research found a way to prevent the Strains from influencing objects by encasing them in silver . . . like the wristbands the guards wear to protect from Strains attacks."

Leilani raised her eyebrows. "You can use the Strains as weapons?"

"Not directly, but have you seen how the Strains can help to lift and throw things? Imagine someone using them to hurl boulders at helpless guards, or to throw the guards themselves. Anyway, those wristbands repel the Strains."

Leilani squinted at the lock. Could it somehow be involved with the dead spots? She could hear the Strains just fine, even standing next to it. "Why is it locked?" she asked.

"Maybe it's dangerous down there. I think it goes to the tunnel network that connects the manors. Father says they are like a maze and people have been lost down there for weeks at a time, having to live off mushrooms and puddles. I wouldn't get lost, of course. The Strains could lead me out."

Leilani and Zeb walked out into the gray, rainy day. Zeb whispered to the Strains and created an umbrella of swirling air that kept the drops off them as they ran across to the small, brick building that was their destination.

Inside, Leilani couldn't decide where to look first. Before her stood a wall covered in gears, wind-wheels, and glass orbs filled with light. A table sat in the middle of the room, holding an apparatus of twitchy arms tipped with pens. These made shaky lines on a long strip of paper. Glass tubes ending in funnels hung from the ceiling. A few young people stood about the room, writing in notebooks.

"Welcome. You must be my new junior fellow." A man with a short, golden beard and bright green eyes strode around the table and put out his hand to Zeb. He wore a brown leather vest and trousers with a white, button down shirt. "Calia . . . Mistress Straight, that is, said she had assigned me the most talented of the new juniors, and she is hard to impress."

"My name is Zebedy Brightly, sir, and this is my aide, Leilani Weaver."

He shook Zeb's hand then Leilani's. "I heard you requested a specific aide. That suggests a special kind of attention to detail. Most juniors don't give it a second thought, but a skilled aide can make all the difference in your early career. It's good to have someone you can trust."

"I do." Zeb beamed.

Fellow Brash motioned towards the table behind him. "Let me show you where we will be focused today." He stepped up to the armed device.

Leilani counted six arms, one for every manor, each writing in a different color of ink.

"This is the audio-strain-o-graph. It measures the strength of the Strains across all the manors." Zeb touched the edge of the device.

"Yes." Brash raised the brown table skirt, revealing bundles of wires disappearing into a hole in the floor. "Each of these runs through the tunnel systems to the sensor I have in place under each manor. The data is relayed back to my instruments via vibrations. The jumps in the line indicate the strengths of the Strains at any given time."

Leilani glanced over the graph. Sometimes the line had only gentle ripples, other times extreme peaks. However, there were no segments of "flat line", no indication of dead spots.

Zeb motioned towards the lines. "Research, Healing, Civics, Art, Weather, and Industry. You know, the Strains are the strongest in the silence of the country. Have you ever measured them there?"

Brash grinned. "No, but only because the machine is near impossible to move, and I haven't devised a way to stretch the lines that far. I am working on a smaller version. Hopefully that will be more portable. Do you want to see it?"

"Oh yes! Leilani, can you take notes?"

Leilani reached into her messenger bag filled with everything Zeb had insisted she would need. She dug past measuring tapes, light tubes, tightly capped bottles of colored ink, and other assorted odds and ends, and found a thick, cloth-bound notebook and a black markstone writing stick.

When Zeb had explained that taking notes made up the majority of an aide's responsibilities, Leilani had been relieved. Her grandmother had schooled her in both calligraphy and shorthand, and she often wrote down orders for her father. If she could keep up with the fast talking master of the tailor shop down the street, she could handle Zeb.

Brash pulled out a small service cart from under the table. Upon this rested a brown leather case with a long strap. Several black enameled knobs and two dials with twitching hands protruded from the top. A hose with a funnel on the end snaked out of it.

Zeb's mouth formed a silent "o."

Leilani squinted at the thing, carefully but quickly sketching the outline into her book. She supposed it was interesting, but this seemed like such a technical way to think of the Strains, measuring and monitoring rather than interacting with them.

Zeb, of all people, should know they were so much more than scientific data. However, that didn't stop her from gasping in delight when Brash exhibited his invention. "Look, Leilani, it reads both pitch and volume. You use the extension to narrow the data, right?"

"Yes. If all the Strains in any given space rushed into this tiny machine, it would shatter a tube. It only analyzes what comes through here." He swung the funnel tip towards Zeb.

The Strains warbled. The hands on the dials vacillated wildly then buried themselves against the far side of the scale.

"By the Strains," Brash whispered. "It's like they are bouncing off you." His brow furrowed then his eyes lit up. "Miss Brightly, I have never seen anyone show such magnetism where the Strains are concerned. This will be a very profitable fellowship for the both of us."

Zeb blushed.

Leilani resisted the urge to roll her eyes. The last thing her friend needed was to have her ego stroked.

Zeb fiddled with her braid. "The Strains are the main reason I joined Research. I'm fascinated with all the music they make, the way they seem to sound differently to everyone I speak to. I sometimes wonder if this is because we are different or if the Strains are different to us. Has there ever been a study about what various sorts of people hear?"

"As a matter of fact, I worked on something similar to that last year." Brash looked around then called out, "Kasan!"

A young man, nearer Leilani's age than Brash's, hurried forward, carrying a notebook. He had dirty blonde hair, so fine and limp it almost appeared gray, and wide-open dark eyes.

"This is Kasan Morgan. Like you, Miss Brightly, I handpicked my aide. Trust is everything in the manors. Kasan, could you show Miss Brightly the study we did on Strain audiology and acoustics? Just take them into the file room."

Kasan bowed at the waist then motioned for the girls to follow him.

The file room turned out to be a glorified closet packed from floor to ceiling with large metal drawers. Leilani squeezed close to Zeb to allow Kasan to roll one open.

"It's alphabetical by subject. Brash's interests span a great number of topics, from Strain detection to the migration patterns of birds." Kasan laughed. He had a high, quaking voice, and his slight frame quivered as he spoke. His fingers danced over the files before lighting on one and drawing it out. "Ah, his study on the growth of the Gelian feather fern. This was the first project we worked together. Did you know that the feather fern reacts to the Strains?"

Leilani didn't, but didn't particularly care. Her eyes wandered over the file and settled on the date, not even four years before.

"You haven't been Fellow Brash's aide long, have you?" she asked.

Kasan's cheeks flushed. "No, but we've known each other since . . . forever. My brother was assigned to be his aide. When he died, Brash wanted to make sure I was looked after. He's been like a brother and father as well as an employer."

"That's sweet," Zeb said. "It looks like you've done some interesting studies together."

Interesting is relative, Leilani thought, glancing over the plant growth statistics.

"Yes, I'm quite fortunate in my employment. It's an honor for one of the Common like me to be an aide. Here are the files you want, a study on the different sounds reportedly made by the Strains." He handed her a folder from the back of the drawer.

Leilani winced. *An honor? I don't know if I'd call it that.*

Zeb opened the folder, and Leilani peered over her shoulder. The report consisted of pie and line graphs tracking various sounds. Some were familiar–like male voices, female voices, birdsong, instruments–and some, like laughter and shrieking, Leilani had never heard of.

"Can you imagine the Strains screaming at you? That would be maddening," she whispered.

Zeb's fingers tightened on the file until the paper wrinkled. "Not as maddening as not hearing them at all. There isn't anything here about who reported which sounds, however. Like male or female, division by age or choice of manor."

Kasan nodded."That is correct. The study participants were

guaranteed anonymity."

Zeb closed the file with a sigh. "It isn't exactly what I was looking for. Maybe that study has never been done."

"Yet."

The girls turned and found Brash smiling at them from the doorway.

"That's the good thing about research. Eventually everything goes under the magnifying glass."

Chapter Nine

After dinner that night, Leilani wandered the halls of the manor. She flexed the fingers of her right hand over and over again. Who knew writing could be so painful? When they had finally retired to their apartment, Zeb had complimented her note taking. Leilani had chosen to use Rynaran shorthand, a lettering system she found to be more efficient than the wispy, curly Gelian script. Zeb had learned it within the few months of their friendship, so they could pass "secret" messages.

"I love it. No one else will be able to read my notes," Zeb chortled. "I want to read them all now!"

Leilani furrowed her brows. "Why? You were there. I didn't write down anything you didn't hear."

Zeb rolled her eyes and poured over the book anyway.

Watching her friend read had swiftly grown boring, so Leilani explored. Perhaps she could find another of those mysterious dead spots. She wanted to know what caused the one they had encountered.

She wandered up and down the halls, reading plaques, peeking through open doors, passing a few servants and some Highmost. The Strains accompanied her the whole time, sometimes quiet but never silent. If not for Zeb's virulent reaction to the dead spot, Leilani would've dismissed it, but the memory of her friend's stricken face still chilled her.

The hallways formed a wide circle about the Observatory. Other passages crossed through them, radiating outward like spokes on a wheel. She passed the locked gate from earlier and stopped. Approaching the closed stairway, she touched the silver lock. Strain-proof. Perhaps the cause of the dead spot involved imbued silver. Leilani shook her head. Speculation was Zeb's expertise. Leilani liked certainties. While coaxing the

Strains to prod at the locking mechanism proved futile, they still danced about her, unaffected by its presence.

No, this silver was not the cause of the dead spot. Not on its own, anyway.

The challenge of the Strain-proof lock still intrigued her. Her grandmother had grown up without the Strains and knew how to complete many tasks without them. Tasks like picking the cupboard lock when she had lost the key.

"Never use the Strains for something you can learn to do with your hands, my little bird," she often said.

Looking about and finding herself alone, Leilani slipped a long, copper pin from her hair. A few strands fell from her bun into her face. She blew them out of her eyes and poked around in the keyhole.

The Strains hummed like angry bees, but for once she ignored them.

"I'm not doing anything wrong. No one will get hurt, anyway." Leilani tried to soothe them like Zeb did. "I just want to see if I can do it. That's all." Their buzzing went up in pitch. Placing her ear to the lock, she listened to the clicks as the pin nudged at the tumblers. She could do this!

The Strains shrieked, an atypically discordant note. Leilani dropped the pin and turned on her heels. Her gaze met the wide-eyed stare of the young deaf guard from the day before. He stood, half in, half out of a doorway about a dozen feet away, his body in shadow but torchlight revealing his youthful face. Leilani's cheeks warmed. He was *watching* her. The young man fled.

Heart pounding, Leilani took off in the opposite direction. What if he told someone? Picking a lock had to be against the law. Oh, she couldn't go to jail, and her parents couldn't afford a fine. What had she been thinking?

She reached her quarters, darted inside, and slammed the door behind her.

Zeb looked up. "Oh, you're back." She closed the

notebook, but not before Leilani had seen the lines of script in Zeb's cramped shorthand. She had been expanding on Leilani's notes. Ink stained her fingers and a pen lay behind her ear. "Your notes are good. Very detailed. I knew you'd have a knack for this. Anyway, you remember how Fellow Brash said the Strains reacted differently to me? It got me to thinking, perhaps they react differently to everyone. I mean, we are all trapped in our own heads, like islands trying to communicate by carrier pigeons . . . or something.

"What if the Strains work uniquely with every individual? How would we even know? It's like colors. Do you ever wonder if everyone sees blue the same way? What if blue is green to you, but you never knew because to you green has always been blue. Blue could be different for *everyone*, and we'd never know. The Strains could be the same way."

Leilani exhaled. She didn't want to talk about this. She knew Zeb didn't understand, but it irked Leilani thinking about how many beautiful voices Zeb could hear that she couldn't. Still, she made herself answer calmly. "Well, of course the Strains are different for you. You're Highmost. You hear voices. I just hear . . . sounds."

Zeb frowned. "I know, but you hear all sorts of sounds, and some people only hear one sort." She slipped her fountain pen from behind her ear and bit the end of it. She started to write again. A black smudge remained on her lower lip.

Leilani hid a laugh with her hand. "Here." She fished out a handkerchief and reached down to dab her friend's mouth.

Zeb put out her tongue, touched the smear with it, and grimaced. "Oh, I did it again. I am glad you're here. Imagine if you weren't. I'd go around with blacked out teeth and twenty pens stuck in my hair." She giggled and flipped through her notes. "I wrote a lot. How long were you gone?"

Leilani shrugged and sat cross-legged on her bed. "I don't know. A while. I wanted to explore."

Zeb opened the book to a sketch Leilani had done of the

portable-strain-detector-thing. "This is a good drawing, but your labeling is ridiculous. 'Twitchy hand dial A and twitchy hand dial B'? Seriously? This is volume and this is pitch." She put a line through Leilani's labels and added her own.

Leilani cleared her throat. "Zeb, have you considered mentioning the dead spot to Fellow Brash? If anyone knows anything about it, you'd think he would. He studies the Strains."

Zebedy bit her bottom lip. "But if he can't explain it . . . Leilani, people can lose the Strains."

"You mean like if you kill someone? Like the Wordless?"

"That is the *usual* way, but there are others. Sometimes as you get older your hearing can suffer and effectively rob you of the gift."

Leilani forced herself not to chuckle. "Zeb, you are not going deaf. I couldn't hear them in the dead spot, either, remember?"

Zeb avoided her friend's eyes. "It's different for you. The Strains are everything to me. I'd go mad without them."

Zeb's words poked into Leilani's chest like needles. "So because I am Common I can't understand?"

"No, because you aren't *me*. Not every Highmost befriends the Strains. Most just use them and don't give it a second thought. The Strains are my family, Leilani. They are an extension of my soul. I've never met anyone who understands that, not even my parents. Fellow Brash does, though. What if he won't work with me because of the dead spot? Because I couldn't hear them for a moment."

Leilani frowned at her friend. Zebedy was the inquisitive one, the one with a thousand questions about everything. Leilani couldn't comprehend how she could let a mystery go so easily.

Zeb stuck her pen back into her hair. "I should go to bed. I told Fellow Brash about my research, about people hearing the Strains differently. He wants me to interview junior fellows from all the manors and see if different specialties attract listeners of different sorts. It's a privilege for me to pick my own project for my second day."

"I'm tired, anyway." Leilani stepped behind the paper privacy screen she had brought from home. With Keris married and Leilani gone, her parents hadn't needed it any more. She slipped out of her uniform and into a white cotton nightshirt and loose bloomers. When she emerged, Zeb had changed into a long nightgown and corralled her flyaway hair into a tight braid. She handed Leilani back her journal.

"Maybe after I've been here a little longer, Fellow Brash will trust me enough to lend me the strain-o-graph. If I can find the dead spot and measure, maybe the Strains were just really quiet, not gone."

"That sounds like a plan."

At least it's something.

Zebedy slipped into her bed and lowered the wick on the lamp until it glowed a soft red. Leilani tucked herself in and turned towards the wall, preferring the darkness. The Strains had a new sound tonight, like water flowing over tinkling crystal. Even though she was Common, Leilani couldn't imagine a world without them. She wished Zeb understood that.

Chapter Ten

The next morning Leilani followed Zeb from manor to manor and listened to young Highmost describe the Strains. The answers were markedly different. While all Highmost seemed to hear the verbal component that Leilani never had, many put more stock in the musical qualities. Some claimed the Strains were represented by a single instrument. A few said it wasn't music at all but more natural noise, like wind through the leaves or rainfall.

One wild eyed youth at the Art Manor reported that the Strains never stopped laughing, and he didn't particularly like it.

Leilani was glad to be out of the Research Manor for a bit. The guard from the night before had been on duty, and when she spied him in the hallway, her heart stopped and her face turned red. He had smiled and winked at her. She wondered why. Was he not going to tell anyone? Reporting–or arresting–someone for breaking and entering seemed like what a guard should do. Why smile when he probably thought her a criminal? The Strains' mood didn't match her own, which was also disturbing. When she saw him, they gave out a happy, playful sound, almost like a child laughing. Even hours later, they sounded like merry frogs croaking in spring time. Leilani wished they'd choose something more calming, but they always had minds of their own.

"Civics next." Zeb's face pinched, her nose wrinkling like a sneezing cat's.

"They can't all be like Vicky," Leilani said.

"One thing you learn growing up in the manors: different specialties attract specific personality types until we're all living like flowers in a garden: the pink blooms in one bed, the blues in another. Civics attracts number crunchers, linear thinkers, little Vickys. I bet they hear the Strains in minor keys."

Leilani glanced down at her notes as they walked towards Civics. "I don't know. Art seemed fairly diversified in the way its fellows hear the Strains."

"That's Art. They get all the odd ones."

Past the grand entrance to the Civics Manor lay a wide, open foyer, shadowed by marble pillars. A small group of junior fellows waited inside, standing in a straight line. Zeb rolled her eyes.

A bearded man strode to meet them. "You must be Zebedy Brightly. Fellow Brash told me you'd be coming. I asked among the junior fellows for volunteers. Hopefully, eight will be a large enough sample."

"Thank you. This is very organized. It won't take long."

The man departed.

Zeb pointed to a long, marble bench against the wall. "Please sit down, and I'll interview you one at a time. I want to be sure you aren't subconsciously influencing each other's responses, so please, do not discuss your answers amongst yourselves. Why don't we start with the young lady on the right."

The other junior fellows filed over to the bench, and Leilani and Zeb took the girl across the room, to an alcove office with an empty desk. Leilani opened her notebook to a fresh page and reached into her bag for her markstone stick.

"Can you list your name and age for me?" Zeb asked.

"Pasha Flats, sixteen," the round faced young woman said. Leilani scribbled this down.

"Thank you, Miss Flats." Zeb drew herself up taller. "All we need is for you to describe the way the Strains sound to you."

"Oh, I've never thought about that." Pasha bit her bottom lip. "Usually they are voices, but different than other voices, as if they are talking underwater. When they aren't 'speaking' they kind of just bubble, like now. Now they are bubbling."

Leilani stopped to listen. To her the Strains sounded more

like twanging fiddle strings. She then smiled at Zeb. "Not minor chords, then?" she teased.

"What? Oh, no, they are never like that." Pasha furrowed her brow.

A shadow fell across them. Leilani glanced over her shoulder and found a tall, gangly young man with short dark hair and sharp brown eyes. He raised his heavy eyebrows. His wide mouth curled into a mocking grin. Zeb turned, her eyes widened, and her jaw dropped. Leilani caught his gaze. He had gorgeous eyes, the kind that made her want to keep looking.

"Hi there, Whistles," he said in a deep voice that would've been more appropriate for a man ten years older.

Zeb stiffened and her expression became unnaturally bland, as if she were trying very hard not to react to something. "Vicky, it's been awhile."

Leilani averted her stare. The last year certainly had caused some marked improvements.

"I heard you were doing a study of some sort and thought I might volunteer."

"You aren't a junior fellow," Zeb said.

"I didn't realize that was a requirement."

Zeb looked at Leilani who shrugged. Zeb tucked a loose strand of hair behind her ear then crossed her arms. "I suppose data is data. Thank you for your time, Miss Flats."

Pasha bowed her head to Vickers. "Good afternoon, Fellow Buffet."

"Hello, Miss Flats. I will see you at the meeting this afternoon."

Pasha hurried away.

"Meeting?" Leilani asked.

"She's on my project team. Civics Manor has me mapping out portions of the manor tunnels. We're considering renovating them to be navigable again."

Zeb gaped. "You're only in your second year. How do you have a project team already?"

"I'm a promising, hard working member of Civics Manor, that's how."

"You mean your father put in a good word for you." Zeb sniffed.

Vickers frowned. "My father hasn't given my career a second thought since I chose Civics over Healing. Now, this study, what is it about?"

"The Strains." Zeb uncrossed her arms. "How people hear them differently."

He scratched his head. "Not particularly practical. What is the real life application?"

"Knowledge is an end to itself. Do you want to help or not?" She tapped her foot.

"It was just a question. No need to get defensive." He glanced at Leilani. "I remember you. You're the one who found her in the woods that time she wandered off. An aide now?"

Leilani nodded. Her initial reaction to him had quieted. She still found him to be attractive, but his expression was so serious. She couldn't help comparing him to the guard with his sparkling, mischievous eyes. Zeb drew nearer her friend, so close their arms touched, a sullen stare upon Vickers.

"So this study?" He reached into his pocket and took out a pair of wire framed spectacles. He positioned them on his nose, furthering his studious look. Zeb's body shook dramatically enough that Leilani felt it and reached out to steady her.

"All right, state your name and age," Leilani said, hoping to distract from Zebedy's sudden discomfiture.

"You know my name and age."

Zeb narrowed her eyes at him.

He grimaced. "Vickers Buffet, eighteen."

"That is Buffet as in to hit someone repeatedly with a blunt object? Correct?" A smile played about Zeb's mouth.

Vickers smirked at her. "Wouldn't you like to know?"

"Not really. Did you get that, Leilani?"

Leilani quickly scratched out the information. "Vickers

Buffet, eighteen, likes to hit things repeatedly with blunt objects. Check."

Zeb snickered before continuing her questions. "So describe how the Strains sound to you."

Vickers rubbed the back of his neck. "They talk, not a lot, but on occasion when I need them to."

"One voice or many?"

"Just the one, deep voice, gravelly, like an old man. Having multiple voices talking around my head would be maddening. Is that what they sound like to you?"

"This isn't about me." Zeb shook her head even though she had once told Leilani she had identified upwards of twelve different voices in the Strains. "Any other sounds? Music?"

"When they don't have anything to say, they just drone, a low buzzing, a bit like music, I guess, but very subtle and in a minor key."

Zeb shot a glance at Leilani who swallowed a grin.

Leilani wrote down the response and looked up. "Is that what they sound like right now?"

"For the most part. They're always a little livelier when she is around. I remember that from our debates." He eyed Zeb, who looked at her feet. He stepped closer to her. "It has been a long time since our initial squabble. I've been meaning to extend an olive branch."

"I don't carry grudges," Zeb said.

Liar, Leilani thought. "That's all we need for the study," she said, hoping to end the interaction before it became awkward.

Vickers shifted his gaze from Zebedy. "I suppose I should let you get back to work then. Maybe we'll run into each other again soon, but if you need anything, you know where to find me." As he spoke his eyes wandered back to Zeb. Leilani decided the glasses made him look old. The Strains twittered as he walked away.

Zeb huffed. "The nerve of him. Waltzing in here as if we were old friends."

“Don’t tell me he’s still your nemesis.” Leilani scoffed.

“Perhaps that was a little dramatic of me, but I was young.” Zeb tugged on her braid. “Anyway, we were never friends.” Still her eyes remained on him until he disappeared down the hallway.

“He is kind of good looking, if he keeps the glasses off,” Leilani said.

“No, the glasses are good. They make him look scholarly. I like the glasses.” Zeb’s brow furrowed. “Why are we talking about Vicky like this? A man like him probably picks his girlfriends through mathematical equation. We need to focus.”

Leilani called the next junior fellow over and the study continued.

Chapter Eleven

When they got back to Research Manor, the sun hovered just behind the city walls.

"Dinner will be soon," Leilani said. "Maybe we should turn in our findings tomorrow."

Zeb shook her head. "Fellow Brash keeps late hours. I'm sure he's still in the workshop. We can at least show him what we collected."

They walked up the path towards the workshop. The muffled sounds of raised voices echoed through the door. Leilani stopped. "That sounds like a fight. Maybe we should come back later."

Zeb found toeholds in the brick wall and pulled herself up to peek through a low window. She gasped. "That's Highmost Cogg. Why is he fighting with Fellow Brash?" She leaped down, her face tightening.

"Highmost Cogg?"

"I really need to give you a lecture on manor hierarchy. He is the senior-most fellow and head of Research. Like your guildmasters, I suppose."

"So Brash's boss?" Leilani climbed up to glance inside, ignoring her better instinct to mind her own business. A small, balding man in a brass buttoned long coat had stationed himself right beneath Brash's chin. He glared up through round-lensed glasses. His mouth flapped open and closed.

Leilani eyed the window latch on the other side of the glass. Not Strain-proof. Even beggar magic such as hers would be sufficient here. She coaxed the Strains. The latch jiggled open, and the window raised just a slit.

"You're useless!" Cogg's shrill voice darted through the window. Leilani dropped down and crouched beside Zeb. "All your projects are fluff. You need to focus on what I give you, or what reason do I have to keep you around? Are the amplifiers ready yet?"

"No but–"

"Of course they aren't!" Cogg sounded like a whistling kettle, full of hot air to the bursting point. "Because if they were, I'd have them at my fingertips. What was our deal, Brash?"

"That I would focus on the amplifiers, but sir, people want to see progress. If I don't work on public projects, they'll question–"

"You don't need to concern yourself with the public eye. You are invisible, remember?"

Leilani winced. She didn't even like Brash, and Cogg's words seemed unnecessarily harsh to her. In Common circles, such insults could lead to blows. She glanced at Zeb.

The young Highmost's face shone red, and her fingers clenched. "He shouldn't talk to him like that . . ."

"Next time I'm here, the amplifiers had better be ready. If not, everyone will know how worthless you are. Even if I have to tell them each individually, they'll know." Beside them the door knob twisted.

"Oh, blast! He's coming out." Leilani looked around. A door stop lay beside the path. She darted over and stuck it under the door jamb, wedging it shut.

"By the Manors! What is wrong with this door?"

The girls scampered away and watched from around the corner as Cogg dislodged the obstruction with the Strains, and stomped down the path to the Observatory.

Cold relief swept over Leilani. "Thank the Strains, that's over. Let's get inside," she said.

"Yes, follow me!" Zeb dashed into the workshop.

Leilani's mouth dropped open. "I meant the Observatory." She groaned and hurried after her friend.

Zeb ran up to Brash and placed her hand on his shoulder.

The fellow's eyes widened.

"Miss Brightly? What are you doing here so late?"

Leilani held forth her notes.

"Oh, your research project." Brash rubbed his forehead. "I will look over it tomorrow. Just leave it on my desk."

Zeb drew her hand back but kept peering at her mentor with big, sympathetic eyes. "Are you sure you're all right?"

Brash cleared his throat and looked away. "You heard my dressing down, didn't you?" He gave a half-hearted laugh.

"He shouldn't have spoken to you that way." Zeb shook her head 'til her braid swung like a pendulum. "You are a valued member of the manor."

"Thank you for thinking so, but unfortunately, manor politics don't always work in my favor. Highmost Cogg measures a fellow's worth on completion of assigned projects, and mine are desperately behind schedule."

"Perhaps I can help."

"Unfortunately, this isn't something I can pass off to a junior fellow, even one as exceptional as you, Miss Brightly."

Zeb's mouth curled into a slight smile then formed a straight line.

Leilani stepped closer. "What are amplifiers?"

Brash's face reddened, and his mouth hardened. "I am sorry, but I cannot speak about this." He snatched the notepad from Leilani's hands. "You should both leave. Now."

Zeb's face fell. "But–"

"Good night, Miss Brightly." Brash turned away.

Zeb's shoulders slumped. Leilani scowled at Brash's back then reached for Zeb's arm. Zeb shook her off and stalked out of the workshop.

Leilani's breath felt hot. "You know, just because your boss was ill-tempered with you, doesn't mean you should pass it on to Zebedy."

Brash faced her, eyes wide. He didn't speak, so Leilani continued.

"She thinks the world of you, no matter what that bully Cogg thinks, and we were just trying to help. Snapping at Zeb makes you as bad as Cogg."

Brash stroked his beard. "You are outspoken for an aide. Be careful. Not all Highmost are as tolerant as myself. Some expect the Common to respect their betters."

Leilani's face burned. "Betters is a matter of opinion." She rushed out before he could respond. *He's no better than the rest of them. Why does Zeb trust the snob?*

"Hey, Miss!"

Leilani jumped. She glanced back and saw a small framed man leaning around the corner of Brash's workshop. She paused as he ambled forward, looking this way and that. It took a moment to put a name to the face: Brash's aide, the kowtowing fellow with the squeaky voice.

"Kasan, isn't it?"

He smiled and nodded. "May I walk with you for a bit?"

"If you want to," she said. She looked towards the workshop door. Brash didn't emerge. *Good.*

"I didn't catch your name, but I'm not surprised. Aides don't really need names, do we?" Kasan said as they began to walk.

Leilani narrowed her eyes at him, uncertain if he meant it as a joke. His mouth stayed placid, neither frowning nor smiling, which made it impossible for her to reach a conclusion.

"It's Leilani Weaver."

Kasan looked down at his shuffling feet. Leilani suppressed a groan, regretting her decision to walk with him. At this rate she'd never catch up to Zeb.

"A word of advice, you're in the Highmost world now. We Common who are fortunate enough to gain such positions, well, it can be hard to learn how to fit in. You seem to be outspoken. This might not be the best place for you." He glanced up.

Leilani cleared her throat "I think I can make that decision on my own, thank you."

"Well, Highmost tend to see Common aides as charity cases. They let us into their remarkable world, show us their toys and luxuries. If we aren't grateful, we don't last long, and maybe we shouldn't. We're sort of like pets to them, you see? And if we aren't properly obedient, well, Highmost can easily afford more tractable pets."

Leilani's face burned. "Zeb isn't like that. We're friends, not servant and employer and certainly *not* master and pet."

"You think so, and maybe she isn't that way *now,* but I've seen it happen over and over again." They reached the door to the Observatory. "I'll leave you here. Think about what I said. "

"I already have." Leilani allowed herself the dramatic flare of a head toss, even though it reminded her of something Keris would do. She broke into a run, eager to put some space between them

Leilani caught up to Zeb in the hallway. Many other junior fellows filled the passage, but all headed in the opposite direction, towards the dining hall. Leilani's stomach rumbled.

Zeb pushed against the flow and into their room. Leilani had to reach out to stop the door from hitting her in the face. Zeb threw herself, face down, onto her bed.

"He only snapped at you because he was embarrassed. You know that, right?" Leilani sat on her own bed and eased her messenger bag from her shoulder.

"Why did you have to ask him about the amplifiers?" The pillows muffled Zeb's voice, but Leilani still caught the frustration in her words. Leilani drew back. Did Zeb blame her?

"Of course I asked. Weren't you at all curious?"

"Yes, I was curious, but I'm not stupid." Zeb rolled onto her side to glare at Leilani.

"That's up for debate!" Leilani snapped. "We shouldn't have gone in at all. Now he knows we listen at windows like gossiping merchants' wives."

"You opened it."

"You peeked through."

The girls stared each other down for a moment before Zeb blinked. The young Highmost sat up, crossing her legs beneath her.

"You don't understand manor politics. My future depends on whether or not Fellow Brash trusts me. If he trusts me, I get projects. If I complete those tasks, he trusts me with more. We were off to such a good start." She reached back and grabbed the top of her braid, squeezing until her hairline moved back from her eyebrows.

Leilani flexed her toes inside her shoes. The emptiness in her stomach crept up her throat. "Are you hungry? We can still make the evening meal if we hurry."

"I have some crackers stashed for later. You can go ahead." Zeb unplaited her braid and ran her fingers through her wavy hair, avoiding eye contact.

Leilani ambled out the door, not wanting to eat among the Highmost without Zeb. She knew of two other aides who were Common, but most were underachieving Highmost, and none particularly good company. She knew the kitchen staff consisted of Common. She could wander down there and find something to eat.

A flight of stairs and several twisting paths later, she sat at the edge of the sweltering, bustling, odorous kitchen. Like in most areas with a lot of folk, the Strains buzzed, hummed, and twittered as noisily as the people, perhaps talking among themselves. Though most of the food had already made its way to the dining hall, a red cheeked baker tossed her a roll and told her to help herself to a wheel of cheese.

Using the Strains so she didn't have to borrow a knife, she shaved off a few curls of hard, yellow goodness and munched away. The splash of water and clanking of dishes reminded her of home. The room smelled of chicken stock from the simmering pots of bones leftover from dinner. Her mother always boiled the bones after a meal and canned the broth in large, glass jars. She used the Strains to test and tighten the seals, a beggar magic skill Leilani doubted the Highmost would give a second thought.

On the far side of the room, across from the tubs of water and bubbling kettles, lay a long, wooden table. The staff set two large pots and a stack of earthenware bowls upon this. A moment later, a troop of dark uniformed guards filed into the room and ladled themselves bowlfuls of chicken soup. They ate in silence, though occasionally fingers would flash. She hadn't realized there were so many deaf folk in Gelia.

She scanned them, finally finding the guard from earlier. He had his back to her, but she recognized the tangle of brown curls. She touched her own straight dark hair and wondered what his felt like. It looked soft and sleek, the color like polished, dark oak.

She longed to talk to him, as impossible as it might be. She watched the guards' silent communication. Zeb had said you could guess at some of it, if you watched, but their hands moved so quickly that it all blended together. Still, if she could speak both Rynaran and Gelian, she should be able to master their gestures. Of course, that would require a teacher.

The guard set down his bowl and swung his leg up and over the bench, turning so rapidly Leilani didn't have time to avert her eyes. He saw her; she could tell from the look of recognition that flooded his face. Stumbling to her feet, she ran from the kitchen.

She diverted down the first side passage she found, intending to put as many twists and turns between her and him as possible.

A few steps down the darkened hall, silence consumed her, and she froze. Her heart beat loudly. She could hear her own rapid breaths, but outside her body, nothing.

No humming. No twittering. No music.

"Strains?" she whispered, remembering how Zeb called to them. Her voice echoed in the quiet. Her skin crawled. So empty. So lonely. So . . . still. She whirled around and fled back into the main hall, colliding against the chest of the young guard. He put his hands on her shoulders, steadying the both of them, and smiled.

The Strains welled to meet her, a tight, twanging noise like a musician tuning his fiddle. Cool relief swept through her chest. The guard raised his eyebrows and pulled his right hand back to wave. Well, that much she could understand.

Embarrassed and flustered, she swallowed hard. He grinned, like an impudent child, and waved again. At a loss for what to do, she returned the gesture.

He glanced about, motioned to the wall, and drew her closer to it. He touched a single brick, traced it with his fingers, then tapped his chest. He then pointed to her, shrugging his shoulders and raising his eyebrows.

She held up her hands. "I'm sorry. I don't . . . I mean, I can't . . . What do you want? Why are you always looking at me? Why don't you . . ."

The young man backed up a step, his mouth forming an "o." A mix between a cough and a gasp, escaped him.

She clenched her fists to stop her fingers from shaking. "Oh Strains. I'm shrieking, and you can't understand a word of it. Am I going mad?"

"Actually, he probably got the gist of it." A calm, laughing voice startled her.

A craggy faced man in a guard's uniform stepped out of the bright kitchen into the shadowy, lantern lit hall.

"Reading lips isn't an exact science, but since Brick's mother isn't deaf, he has practice."

She glanced at the young man who nodded, his smile now sheepish.

"Brick? That's your name?" Leilani asked. "Oh, so that's . . . I'm sorry. I'm Leilani. But I still don't understand why you've been watching me. It's unnerving."

"Well, Brick?" The older man raised his hands, palms up.

Brick turned red, pointed to Leilani, and circled his face

with his open hand, over his eyes and then down to a warm smile. The other guard laughed.

"What did he say?" Leilani asked.

"He'll explain later. It isn't my business. Brick, get back to the barracks." The older guard used his fingers and arms to communicate even as he spoke. Brick bowed to her then marched off down the hall. Leilani bit her bottom lip, a mix between relief and regret stirring in her chest.

"I'm Captain Goodly, commander of the Research Manor Guards. I am sorry Brick upset you. That wasn't his intention."

She looked after Brick then back to Goodly. "You aren't deaf."

His smile grew sad. "No, I'm Wordless. At one point, I was Highmost."

Her face went cold. "You're Wordless as in . . . you've killed someone?"

"Unfortunately, the Strains don't judge motive. Many years ago, when I was a junior fellow in Industry, a highwayman put me in a position where my choices were death or defense. I chose defense. There were times in the days after that I regretted it. I lost my fellowship, my friends abandoned me, and the silence was deafening."

Leilani shifted her feet. "The Strains abandoned you? For protecting yourself? That seems so unfair."

"I thought so at first, but after some time, I realized it is their protection against misuse. Imagine the havoc the Highmost could unleash if they could use the Strains for violence? Cutting off any who would take a life prevents the Strains from becoming a weapon. Death is death to them, no matter the reasons." He smiled, his old eyes shining. "Besides, there was a reason for it. I found the guard, and they made me one of their own. Brick's grandfather was my mentor. He taught me to sign and helped me find my way and my purpose. The deaf are often overlooked by Highmost and Common alike. I can provide them a voice in the manors.

"The Strains are not everything, Miss Leilani. According to the Holy Scripts, they are but the servants and messengers of a greater power. I never sought communion with such until the lack of Strains drove me to it. Those like Brick taught me how."

Leilani rubbed her chin. She had heard the scripts read on Holy Days, telling of the Maker who sent the Strains to aid His creations, but He was a distant figure. The Strains were real and immediate, the Maker intangible and incomprehensible. She rarely gave thought to the Maker, but the Strains she adored.

"Thank you for helping me with Brick," she said. "Would you apologize for me? I shouldn't have yelled at him."

He bowed. "I will. Good night then, Miss Leilani."

Leilani walked back towards her room, avoiding the hall where she had encountered the dead spot.

Chapter Twelve

Zeb didn't return until late, carrying an armful of books. She stayed up until long after Leilani wished to fall asleep, reading and taking notes. Leilani drifted off to the scratching of Zeb's markstone stick on the paper.

At breakfast Zeb had dark circles under her eyes. Her fingers twitched, and she smiled as she ate.

"After you left, I went to the library and found Fellow Brash. He assigned me these books, said it would keep me busy for the next week, and then I'd be ready for a new project. I can't wait to tell him I finished in one night!"

Leilani raised her eyebrows. "Did you even sleep?"

"Yes, a little, enough anyway."

Leilani opened her mouth to chide her friend, but thought better of it and took a bite of muffin instead.

Zeb took coffee rather than her usual milk with breakfast. The fragrance drifted towards Leilani and made her eyes open wider. Zeb took a sip, asked the girl to her left to pass the sugar, then spooned three large scoops into the dark liquid. She sloshed it around, the spoon on the china sounding like a ringing bell. She took a drink then winced. "Too hot. Can I have some of your milk? Just a splash to cool it down."

Leilani passed her the cup. Part of her wanted to tell Zeb what Brash had said about "betters." Zeb had always been quick to defend Leilani against that sort of snobbery, and probably would even if it was from Brash. However, Brash was, for better or worse, Zeb's superior. It would be unwise to cause a rift there. He'd show his true colors eventually. "So you and Fellow Brash are friends again?" she asked.

Zeb nodded and slurped on her coffee. "Yes." She dropped her voice. "He told me Cogg has never liked him, and he doesn't particularly trust Cogg. The man is all about influence. He wants to hold the Highmost Seat, and he's pushing Brash on projects so he can use the results to make his case in the next election. Can you imagine? I don't know why Brash puts up with it. He's one of the most promising fellows. Research can't afford to lose him to, say, Industry or Healing." Zeb stood. "I don't need your help today. Brash wanted to talk about the books, and I would rather it be one on one. We'll be busy until this afternoon. You should explore a bit."

Leilani scraped the last bite of her porridge from her bowl. "If that's what you want, I suppose I will see you after lunch."

A free day, even a half day, was unheard of in Common circles. Other than Holy Days and festivals, work came first. With Zeb not needing, or at least not wanting, her, Leilani couldn't decide what to do.

She paced along the outside of the Observatory, enjoying the sunshine. The air had a crisp chill to it. Soon the Gelian canals would freeze over and snow would fall. She wrapped her cloak close. Ahead lay the long, rectangular barracks. The gate swung open, and Brick emerged, wearing a plain brown tunic and leggings instead of his uniform. He didn't look towards her but turned onto the path leading to the main road. His arms swung easily at his sides, and his steps had energy, like each one had a purpose, but also a pleasure.

Her mouth quirked. She would show him he wasn't the only one who could play spy. Casting her hood over her brow, she followed after him. She imagined glaring at him when he realized he was being watched then stomping away, her point made.

Brick left Research and strode along the busy road. When they came to the Art Manor, he took the path through the gate, gazing up at the abstract creations that lined the way.

From her trip there, interviewing junior fellows with Zeb, Leilani knew that the lower floor of the Art Manor was open to the public. Various artists displayed their work here, even

Common craftsmen. Art encompassed a large variety of disciplines, from painting and sculpture to weaving and embroidery. Leilani tailed Brick into the building, past paintings and tapestries.

Brick strolled among the masterpieces. Every so often he stopped and stared. She paused in her pursuit. She hadn't expected him to come here, just to sight-see among the paintings.

He settled on a bench in front of a marble carving of a leaping stag. He leaned forward, his hands on his knees, his eyes traveling up and down the artwork.

Leilani wished she could ask him what he was thinking. Perhaps she should leave. Following him had been a foolish idea.

The Strains murmured in her ear, a wordless whisper, gentle and soothing. The sound relaxed her, and she sighed. She moved one foot forward, towards him, then back again. No, she should go. Spying on him was silly, not clever.

Without warning, Brick looked up. He smiled and waved. She blushed and pushed her hood away from her face. Obviously the disguise was inadequate. He patted the empty spot on the bench beside him. She shuffled over and took a seat.

"Hi. Brick, right?"

His eyes stayed intently on her lips as she spoke. He nodded.

She glanced at the statue. The creature did look lifelike, though the color of the white stone made the beast resemble a ghost, a frozen phantom of a deer rather than a living creature.

Brick stood. He ran his fingers along the statue's back in a sweeping motion. He offered Leilani his hand. She took it and stood. He led her around the piece in a slow circuit, pointing at details: the delicate lines on the stag's hooves; the flare of its nostrils. His movements traced the creature but rarely touched it. There was an elegance to his appreciation, like the marble itself.

"You really like it, don't you?" she asked.

He nodded. He circled his face with his palm, a warm smile on his face. The same signal he'd made towards her the day before. He pointed to the statue. Leilani duplicated his gesture, her hand going from her eyes to her smile.

Something he saw that made him smile . . .

She blushed.

"Beautiful?" she asked. His smile broadened, and he nodded again.

Leilani dropped her eyes. No one, outside her family, had ever called her beautiful before. It just wasn't how she thought of herself. She was practical, strong, feisty . . . beautiful, though, that word belonged to her mother or Keris, Zeb even, but not Leilani. Maybe she had misunderstood. His eyes twinkled at her, and she smiled at him.

He had an expressive face, easy to read and ever changing. His whole presence radiated cheer and ease, and the feelings seeped into her own bones.

The Strains caught the mood and whistled like nesting robins.

"I wish I knew your language," she said.

He still held her hand as they walked to the next display, this one a tapestry with a pastoral scene. His fingers felt warm and safe. She liked it. He glanced at her; realizing he had been looking away when she spoke the first time, she repeated the phrase.

One corner of his mouth quirked. He rubbed his stomach then raised his eyebrows and pointed to her belly. Confused, she mimicked him. The gesture stirred a memory.

"Oh, am I hungry?"

He smiled and nodded.

She hesitated. Not particularly, but if he was, she could eat. Not confident that she could express an idea more complicated than yes or no, she rubbed her stomach and bobbed her head, "Yes."

They exited the Art Manor and walked along the main road together. Leilani blushed when they passed other folk, for Brick still clasped her hand. No one gave them a second look, however, and soon she held her head up, beaming at his public affection.

In the side street between Art and Civics lay a small group of shops, including several cart vendors selling foodstuffs. Brick waved his hand at the line of them. When Leilani didn't move, he motioned again.

"Oh!" She pointed to a cart serving paper bags of fried fish and thinly sliced potatoes. Brick grinned and gave her a thumbs up. He left to make the purchase, and she found a bench to sit on.

Her heart fluttered like a moth against her rib cage. What was happening? What was going to happen? She watched him with inexplicable fascination. His every movement, every change of expression, sent a quiver through her. She felt hot and cold and breathless and happy. She couldn't remember the last time she had been so happy.

He returned with two paper bags and passed her one.

"Thank you. How do you say 'thank you?'"

He made a fist and tapped his chest over his heart. She did the same. She took a crispy potato and tried to nibble daintily. Brick snatched up a handful and popped them into his mouth. He wiped his greasy fingers on his pant leg.

They ate in silence, for what choice did they have? Every so often a question would bubble to the surface. She would mull over ways to convey the idea then debate whether or not she could comprehend the possible responses. She never spoke.

He finished the last bite of his meal, and together they rose, her still snacking on the crisp potatoes, him clutching his crumpled, empty bag. She supposed it wouldn't be appropriate for a guard to litter.

They walked, no longer holding hands, back out to the

main street. At the crossroads he hesitated, looking left, then right. He glanced down at her and shrugged. She bit her bottom lip. There had to be some way around the lack of communication.

She hesitated. She still had her messenger bag tucked under her cloak, though she'd left a lot of Zeb's "necessities" at home, making it blessedly lighter. She opened the flap and rustled for her markstone stick and a spare notepad. His eyes lit up when he saw them. He motioned one way then the other and raised his eyebrows. She scratched out, "Do you want to go to the Botanical Gardens?"

He nodded and, once again taking her hand, led the way towards the Leisure District.

§

When she got back to Research, Leilani felt lighter somehow, as if all the troubles of the last few days had evaporated. She found Zeb in the library, studying again.

Zeb eyed her. "What have you been up to?"

Leilani shrugged. "I just went for a walk in the gardens. It's a beautiful day."

"Really? I thought it was rather cold out." Zeb handed her a book. "Here, I need you to read through and copy any sections that involve the effects of Strains on plant growth . . . or if it is a long section, just write down the page number so I can find them easily. It'll streamline my study process."

Leilani grimaced as she took the book. It was a dull task, but she supposed that was what she signed up for, and Zeb appeared to be doing roughly the same thing. The girls sat in silence for the remainder of the afternoon.

§

The next day at lunch, a waitress slipped Leilani a note.

"What's that?" Zeb asked as the girl winked at Leilani and hurried away. Recognizing the handwriting, Leilani blushed.

"Just a note from a friend I met yesterday," she said, not ready to tell Zeb about Brick.

"Oh. It's good that you're making friends. Is she a junior fellow or another aide?" Zeb took a bite of bread.

"Neither, just Common like me." For a moment Leilani thought she saw disappointment in Zeb's eyes, but it faded. "I'm not hungry. Do you want me to go ahead to the workshop? See what Brash wants from you this afternoon?"

Zeb shook her head. "He's taking a long lunch with Mistress Straight. He's rather flirty with her. I'm beginning to think it's his default manner with females. I'm going to get some reading done in our room. Why don't you go see your friend? Ask if she wants to join us for dinner sometime."

Leilani nodded and slipped away. She opened the note in the first stretch of empty hallway.

Hello, Lei,

Yesterday was fun. I knew I'd like you when I saw you picking that lock. Something just clicked in my head, and I thought, 'This is a girl who takes chances and doesn't let obstacles stand in her way.' I like that. You don't see enough of that in the manors.

I hope I can see you today, but I have back to back watches. If you have time, I am free for a few hours around lunch and will be in the barracks. Hope I can find someone to bring you this message.

See you soon,

Brick

She smiled. The Strains piped like flutes, a happy, playful melody, a bit erratic, but it matched her heartbeat. Walking as fast as she could without drawing attention to herself, she hurried through Research.

The door to the guard's quarters was wide open. Two older guards leaned beside it, smoking pipes and chatting.

They obviously aren't deaf like Brick. Are they Wordless, like Goodly? I suppose it would be impolite to ask.

She opened her mouth to explain, but the older of the two just smiled and waved her in.

Wow, I'm expected. I wonder what he told them.

The barracks was one large room lined with at least two dozen cots, each with a small footlocker at the end. Brick sat about halfway down the row, polishing his boots. He grinned and beckoned her closer.

She sat on the cot across from him and held out the note. His face turned a shade pinker, but his smile remained.

"You say such nice things. I'm glad we're friends," she said.

His eyes clouded. He took up a notepad then rummaged around on the floor before shrugging and pointing towards her mouth.

"Oh . . . we're friends. Me, you." She pointed from herself to himself. "Friends."

He nodded. Holding out both hands, he made circles with his index fingers and thumbs and locked his hands together so that his fingers looked like chain links.

"Friends?" she asked.

He took her hands and helped her form the same shape.

She repeated the gesture. "Friends."

His smile widened, and he let out a long, loud, "Ah!"

Startled, her hands dropped.

Brick flushed and looked away. The Strains gave a low whistle and died down to a depressing dirge of organ music.

"Oh no. Don't . . ." She stood. Glancing down she spied a markstone stick poking out from under his polishing cloth.

Oh, that's what he was looking for. She picked it up and passed it to him.

He took a minute writing, obviously considering his words carefully.

I'm sorry. I forget how strange I must sound. When I was younger, littler kids were scared by how I sounded. I didn't quite understand why, but I realized they accepted me easier if I just stayed silent. Sometimes it just slips out, though. So sorry I scared you.

She shook her head and took the notepad.

I wasn't scared. Just surprised. I stupidly thought you couldn't make sounds at all. Please never apologize for who you are. I like who you are. Who you are makes me smile.

He let out a long breath as he read her note. His hand stroked the side of her face, making her breath catch in her throat. He repeated the sign, *friends,* his lips quirking into a half smile. For a moment a strange desire to kiss him filled her, and she had to look away from his mouth.

She wrote out another note. **My father is a weaver. Is your dad a guard too?**

He shook his head and took the pad. **He was a handyman at Healing Manor. My grandfather was a guard though.**

She noted the 'was' and her face warmed. "Is he dead?" seemed a rude thing to ask, so she changed the subject. **Do you like being a guard?**

For an instant his mouth quirked downward. **It puts bread on the table. What about you? How come you're in the manors, not a weaving shop?**

As she took her turn with the markstone stick, the Strains started a merry tune, mirroring her current mood. Part of her wished Brick could hear them, but she pushed the thought out of mind and kept writing.

Chapter Thirteen

They exchanged notes for over an hour before Brick pulled out a dented pocket watch, checked the time, then tucked it away again.

He scratched out in his large, blocky letters: **I need to get back for my shift, but if we leave now I can walk you home.**

He stuck out his elbow, allowing her to slip her arm through the crook in his.

They passed few people, for most of the fellows worked in outside workshops, like Brash's. When they reached the hallway outside her and Zeb's quarters, however, Leilani released Brick's arm, her hands dropping to her sides.

Zeb sat, huddled in front of their door, her hair disheveled and her knees pulled against her chest.

"Zeb? What's wrong?" Leilani rushed to her friend's side and put her hand on the door knob, hoping to get her out of the hall.

I can't let her be seen like this.

"No!" Zeb's hand shot up and pulled Leilani's from the handle.

Leilani stared down at her. The black of Zeb's pupils widened to consume the cloudy sky blue of her eyes.

"The dead spot is in there." Zeb whimpered. "It's in my home. Oh Leilani, what if I am cursed? What if it is after me?" She shrank into Leilani's chest, shuddering.

Leilani felt a soft touch on her shoulder and looked up to see Brick. He pointed to Zeb, then forced his face into an exaggerated frown, and traced imaginary lines from his eyes. He raised his hands, palms up.

Leilani hesitated. How could she communicate this? Even if he managed to read her lips, he had never heard the Strains.

Would he understand?

"She's frightened," Leilani said. "It's hard to explain."

Zeb pried her face from Leilani's shoulder and stared at Brick. "Who are you?"

He waved and nodded to Leilani.

"This is Brick. He's a guard and . . . my friend."

Brick's mouth curled into an unruly grin. He hooked his thumbs together and mouthed, "Friend" then raised his eyebrows.

Zeb blinked at him, pursing her lips. She waved and turned back to Leilani. "I can't go in my room if the Strains aren't there."

"The dead spots always fade. It's probably already gone. Here." Leilani untangled herself from Zeb's embrace. Zeb scooted across the hallway, her rump never leaving the floor, as Leilani opened the door and stepped into the room.

The silence hit her like the slap of an icy hand. Resisting the urge to flee, she steadied herself against the door frame.

Zeb's love of collecting and analyzing information had never rubbed off on Leilani. It simply didn't seem a useful pursuit. However, in this situation it was exactly what was needed.

But Zeb wouldn't move.

She turned to look at her friend. Brick had stationed himself at Zeb's side though his eyes squinted in puzzlement.

"Zeb, we can figure this out. You are good at deduction and observation. Help me get to the bottom of this."

Zeb dropped her gaze and didn't speak. Her hands clenched and unclenched, her knuckles as white as her face.

Leilani exhaled her frustration. She forced herself further into the room. Standing in the narrow space between the two beds, she listened. So silent. So unnerving. Only the drumming of her heart.

It wasn't just the quiet, however. The air felt thin and substance-less, as if something had been drained from it. An image of the dried fruit her mother made sprang to mind. The air resembled those, wrung out and condensed, wrinkled husks of themselves.

Chills danced up and down her spine. She returned to Zeb and helped her stand.

"How long ago did you find it?" Leilani asked.

"Right after lunch. I'm not sure how long it has been. It feels like hours."

Leilani frowned. It *had* been at least an hour. The spots had never lasted this long before. Things were getting worse.

Leilani touched Brick's arm. "You should go or you'll be late for your shift. Thank you for the wonderful time."

He smiled again, linked his thumbs together, then waved.

"Good-bye 'friend' to you too." She laughed.

She watched him until his head disappeared over the horizon of the staircase.

Zeb rubbed her arms as if trying to warm herself. "What now?"

"I don't know." Leilani shrugged. "There is a massive, silent dead spot hovering in our room. I won't be able to sleep in there tonight. Will you?"

"Oh Strains, no." Zeb winced.

They stood, side by side, staring at the doorway.

"Zeb, we should tell someone," Leilani finally said. "We can bring them here and show them and maybe they will know what to do. The Strains have been around for . . .well, ever. Surely someone has heard of dead spots and knows what to do about them. We should go to Mistress Straight or Fellow Brash or even Highmost Cogg."

Zeb shuddered.

Leilani touched her shoulder. "They won't cast you out, not when you can show them. Please. You're falling to pieces."

Zeb nodded. "I think Fellow Brash will still be in the library."

Zebedy led the way down one of the straight spoke-like

halls towards the wheel's center, a round room that stretched upward for three stories. From the middle, on a great, metal turntable that enabled it to face any portion of the sky, jutted the massive telescope. Great, twisting staircases circled this, allowing fellows to reach several viewing platforms where lesser astronomical tools–astrolabes, charts, and planispheres–rested. The roof was domed with great skylights allowing the telescope to gaze outward. The room beneath had a roughly hexagonal shape. Each of the six sides housed shelves crowded with books from floor to ceiling.

A few fellows roamed about or sat, reading, on the benches. Zeb continued past these to a section beneath the telescope. She stopped short.

Brash sat at the table, pouring over papers, and across from him stood Cogg.

No longer red faced, the Highmost of Research at least appeared placid, his mouth frowning, but only slightly, and his eyes dull, rather than blazing. Zeb backed up a step. Leilani put her hand between Zeb's shoulder blades with a gentle push. A swallow rippled down Zeb's throat. Cogg cast his eyes upon them, and his brows melted together. Zeb pressed back into Leilani's hand.

"This is one of your juniors, isn't it, Brash?" Cogg asked.

Brash turned to look at them. "Miss Brightly, I thought you were writing a report this afternoon. Are you finished already?"

"No, sir." Zeb's voice quavered like one of the taut strings of Mr. Weaver's loom. The Strains vibrated in sync with her words. "There is something wrong. We found 'dead spots'."

"Dead spots?" Cogg's face contorted, becoming even more unpleasant. "What nonsense are you spouting?"

"I don't know what to call them. I'd never found one before I came here, but they are like big, empty holes where the Strains have disappeared. The first ones only lasted minutes, but today one settled over our room and won't leave."

Cogg snorted. "Childish nightmares! This is what comes of

coddling the younger generation."

Leilani scowled at the man. Adult or not, High-Whatever or not, he had no right to dismiss Zeb that way, not when she was so obviously frightened. She burrowed her stare into his forehead until he noticed. His jaw slackened for a moment before he hardened his mouth and eyed Brash. "Tell your juniors we have real issues to concern us."

Brash sucked his bottom lip between his teeth. Leilani rolled her eyes. There was no way Brash was man enough to stand up to Cogg or even tell Zeb off. He wanted to play both sides of this game. The Strains whistled around them, maybe trying to coax the men one way or another, but no one reacted to them.

"This *is* real!" Leilani said. "We have found *three* of them so far, and every time they are bigger and last longer."

"What if they grow to consume all the Strains?" Zeb's eyes widened, and she clenched her hands together.

Brash cleared his throat. "Sir, if they are right–"

"Brash! You aren't really buying into this rubbish? I forbid you, any of you–" He swept his glare across both of the girls then hit Brash with a targeted beam of malice. The Strains hummed a rapid, twittering tone. "–to speak of this. You'll cause panic and chaos, and I will not have *my* fellows spreading rumors. The Strains are, have always been, and will always be, stable." Cogg stepped around the table, muttering, "If I wanted to waste my time listening to prattle, I'd attend one of Art's insipid theater productions."

Leilani put her arm around Zeb's slumping shoulders as Cogg stalked off.

"It isn't prattle," Zeb whispered.

Brash stood. "Show me."

The girls led Fellow Brash up to their quarters. Leilani put her hand on the doorknob, for the first time praying that the dead spot would be there.

She stepped in, and her heart sank. The Strains still

whistled about her. Biting her bottom lip, she moved into the center of the room. Absolute quiet encircled her. Her skin prickled, and she turned and beckoned to Brash.

The fellow walked to her and nodded. "I've never experienced anything like this."

Leilani looked past him to where Zeb cowered against the opposite wall. "Zeb, it is shrinking. That means it will be gone soon. Come on."

Zebedy came forward with timorous steps. She stood at the foot of her bed.

The Strains trickled back into the dead spot like water filling a vessel. They sounded subdued, but after the silence, any sound was welcome. Leilani's chest rose and fell freely once more.

"So it is real." Brash scratched the back of his neck.

"And each one has lasted longer than the last," Zeb said. "Please, tell Highmost Cogg. He needs to do something."

Brash's eyes narrowed. "He didn't seem open to this discussion."

"But you've felt it now. He has to listen to you!" Zeb bounced on her toes like a child in need of a chamber pot.

"Surely other folk have encountered these spots," Leilani said. "We've found three spread over Research. Someone else is bound to stumble onto one soon, if they haven't already. Plus if they are lasting for hours at a time, we can show people."

Brash shook his head. "If you try to tell others, even with proof, Cogg will have you evicted. He doesn't tolerate dissension."

Leilani raised her eyebrows.

Zeb's hairline elevated. "That goes against the very spirit of Research! We are meant to ask questions. Anyway, shouldn't he want to protect the Strains?"

"Unless he has a vested interest in keeping this quiet." Brash motioned towards the door. Leilani shut it, and he sat on the edge of Zeb's bed. "Don't trust Highmost Cogg. I can't explain everything I know, but he looks out only for himself and his own power. If it were to his benefit to somehow . . . harness the Strains, he would do so without a moment's hesitation."

"Harness the Strains?" Leilani glanced at Zeb whose jaw hung slack. "How and why?"

"The project he has me working on, the amplifiers . . . again, I cannot be specific. I have questioned his motives for wanting them built and his need to keep everything secret. His answers have never satisfied me."

"Could the amplifiers create dead spots?" Zeb asked.

Brash shook his head. "No. Strains, no. If anything, they would do the exact opposite. They are called amplifiers for a reason."

Leilani frowned. The Strains hummed in a tight, high pitched tone.

Zeb cleared her throat. "They amplify the Strains. Make them louder."

Leilani flushed. She should've been able to put that together.

"You girls need to step aside. This could be dangerous. Let me handle it, all right? Cogg does not respect me, but he does trust me not to betray him. I should be in a position to find out if he is in some way behind this. In the meantime, lie low, pretend to forget." Brash rose, walked to the door, put his hand on the knob, and looked back over his shoulder. "You've done well, Miss Brightly."

Zeb beamed long after the door had closed behind him. Leilani rolled her eyes, fed up with Zeb's obsession with Brash.

Zeb reached for the notepad on her bedside table. "I'm glad that's over with. Anyway, I've been thinking about the study we did. At all the manors, most junior fellows identified the Strains as having a single voice, with the exception of Healing. Many at Healing reported multiple voices within the Strains, like I do. Fellow Brash suggests that multiple voices mean a Highmost is more empathetic which is why many with that trait end up in Healing. I don't want to leave Research, but he gave me a few books on Healing, just to pique my interest."

Leilani gaped at her friend. "Zeb, seriously? Over with? How can you just pass this off to Brash and leave so many questions unanswered? For all we know, he is working with Cogg. Do you really trust him?"

Zeb gave an incredulous cough. "Of course I trust him. Why wouldn't I?"

"Because you just met him." Leilani sat on her bed. "How can you know him?"

"I know him better than you know your *friend*." Zeb scowled. "What are you doing with a Wordless, anyway?"

Leilani's mouth tightened. "He's not 'a Wordless'. He's deaf. There's a difference. Also, his name is Brick, and I like him."

"How can you like him? You can't even communicate, not like you and I can, anyway. How do you even know what he is like?" Zeb's mouth twisted.

"I just know, all right? Besides, do we really want to talk about boys right now? I'm not asking you to trust Brick with something as important as the dead spots."

"Well, maybe if you spent less time gallivanting around with Brick and more time talking with Brash, like I have, you would trust him like I do."

Leilani clenched her fists. "That's not fair. You . . ." She drew a deep breath and let it out through her nose. "Brick is nice and thoughtful. I think you'd like him."

"If it is all the same to you, I'd rather stick with Brash."

"I don't see what is so great about Brash. He's just another stuffy Highmost."

Zeb's eyes clouded. "He's not stuffy. Cogg is stuffy. Brash is my friend. He knows all about manor politics, and he says he'll help me navigate my first few years. I need someone like him. You could learn from him, too, if you wanted. He knows all sorts of things about the Strains and manor history."

"I don't trust him, and you shouldn't either. I'm going to take a walk." Leilani stomped out of the room.

She wanted to tell Zeb about Brash insulting her in his workshop, but in Zeb's current mood, perhaps she'd excuse even that behavior. With Brash, Zeb seemed to have a blind spot. Leilani could've overlooked it if not for the dead spots, though Zeb's dismissal of Brick irked her a good deal.

She listened to the Strains. They jangled now, like a pocketful of coins. Words weren't everything. She could know Brick even if he couldn't speak. He had treated her with courtesy. He liked art and thought it was beautiful. He thought *she* was beautiful.

Her heart palpitated, and she slowed her furious pace. Perhaps she simply disliked hearing Zeb voice her own fears. After all, she had come to care for Brick so quickly. How real could it be? What would it be like to love a man who could never hear her voice?

Love.

The word made her breath quicken. Could it really be happening? To her? Now? No, she couldn't commit to that word, not yet, not even in her own head. Still, she did like him a good deal.

Suddenly longing to see him, she detoured down the hall where they had first met, hoping he had been assigned the same station.

However, a different guard, a few years older than Brick, paced about the circular bench. Leilani's mouth pinched. Sighting her, the guard nodded respectfully.

She walked up to him. "Excuse me, I'm looking for another guard."

The guard grimaced, cupped his hands over his ears, then shrugged. Her stomach twisted. She needed to learn how to communicate with the deaf. She stepped to the wall and beckoned the guard closer. She traced the outline of a single brick, the way Brick had when introducing himself. The guard's face lit up. He pointed down the hallway then to his left twice.

She repeated the motions. "Down there then two left turns?"

He smiled and nodded. Her heart eased. Maybe this was manageable.

Following the guard's directions, she passed the strange gateway with the Strain-proof lock. Brick paced at the far end of the hall. He sighted her and waved. Hurrying forward, he motioned to the gate with a grin. She lowered her gaze bashfully then raised her face so he could see her lips.

"I was curious. I wanted to do something without the Strains."

He took her hand and led her to the gate. Reaching behind her head, he pulled a pin from her bun. As he drew his hand back, it brushed against her cheek. He held up the pin, took the lock in his other hand, then pressed the pin into her palm.

"Really?" She raised her eyebrows. "You want me to pick the lock?"

She inserted the pin into the keyhole and wiggled it around. He watched, his brows slightly wrinkled and a smile playing about his lips. She listened to the clicks and felt the give whenever she hit a tumbler. He chuckled, a little too loudly. She realized he had never heard his own laugh. What would that be like?

She paused in her work. He touched her wrist. She forced a smile, not wanting him to see her doubt.

A satisfying snap rang out, and she froze. Her eyes met Brick's, and he gave her a thumbs up, his eyes twinkling like all the stars in the sky. She felt dizzy. The lock fell open in her hand. The gate swung inward.

Stepping through, she found herself at the top of a tall stair case, descending into utter darkness. The air had an unpleasant scent, like stagnant water. Brick's nose wrinkled. Leilani returned to his side.

Closing the gate, she replaced the lock, not snapping it

shut but letting it rest so it hopefully wouldn't draw anyone's attention. She might wish to come back to it.

She walked up and down the hall with Brick for a bit, keeping him company on his rounds. His presence calmed her until she felt reasonable enough to join Zebedy for dinner.

Zeb ate in silence, occasionally glancing at Leilani. Her mouth turned down and her eyes were drawn. Leilani avoided looking at her and pretended to eat with relish though each bite felt as dry as dust.

They walked back to the room after dinner. Leilani sat on her bed and picked up a book, determined to ignore Zeb indefinitely. Zeb stood above her, clutching her braid.

"Leilani," she said.

Leilani kept her eyes on the page, even though she'd opened it to the wrong chapter. Zeb sighed and lay on her own bed, her arms crossed beneath her head.

Leilani flipped through the book, trying to remember where she had left off. It was a romance, the dry kind where the boy and girl fought for foolish reasons, and she kind of hoped one or both would die before the end. Zeb would read anything, no matter how dull or silly. Leilani had read a few chapters and put it aside, fully intending never to finish it, but it had been within arms length when she needed something to stare at.

"Most Highmost don't marry until their thirties."

Leilani looked up at Zeb's random comment.

"We just don't. You are expected to spend at least two decades fully devoted to your manor before taking time away for marriage and children."

"You've never been one to do the expected." Leilani shut the book.

Zeb sat up. "Your sister was about your age when she married."

"Common marry young. There isn't a reason to wait."

"I thought if you joined me at the manors, that would be your reason. Maybe you'd even meet a Highmost man you liked. Highmost marry Common more than you'd think, especially in the manors like Art and Civics where they interact a lot. Some Highmost even have two kids, not often, but it happens, so maybe we could marry brothers. I could have the older, responsible one, and you could take the younger, fun loving one."

Leilani crossed her legs and leaned forward. Zeb had certainly given that some thought. "I just met Brick. We aren't going to run off together any time soon. Even if we did, he's a guard and works in the manors. I'd still be close to you."

"It wouldn't be the same." Zeb rested her chin in her hands. "Maybe if I married an older man, then we could be married at the same time. I like the responsible, studious type. I wouldn't mind if he were a dozen or so years older, and I'm advanced, so an older man might suit me."

Leilani's brow tightened. "Fellow Brash hasn't been flirting with you, has he? That would be kind of . . . creepy."

Zeb turned red. "No, and I didn't mean Brash. I like him, but he's not very confident. He lets Cogg bully him, and I don't understand why. Plus he's fairer than I prefer."

But she's thought about it. Leilani determined to keep a closer eye on Brash. Zeb could be ridiculously naive, and Leilani wouldn't let anyone take advantage of that.

"I like darker hair too. I think I'd want to pluck Brash's blond beard out if I was forced to look at it every day for the rest of my life." Leilani shrugged.

Zeb giggled. "I suppose your Brick does have very nice hair. I've never seen a boy with curls like that. Most keep it a little shorter . . . it's kind of pretty, but a little too . . . I don't know, not what I want either."

Leilani's face softened. "He's not *my* Brick. We're just friends. He is nice, though, Zeb. I hope you'll give him a chance."

Zeb sighed. "I'll try. For you."

Chapter Fourteen

The next day was business as usual. Leilani helped Zeb finish her paper on their Strains research. Leilani copied it in her neatest script. She used a device in the library where the pen was attached by a metal arm to another pen that moved as she moved the first, creating an exact copy of whatever she wrote. The novelty made the task less tedious.

With a copy for Brash and one for Zeb's portfolio, they returned to the workshop. Brash showed his juniors how to calibrate his strain-o-graphs, first the large one, then the portable version. Seeing these instruments made Leilani long to investigate the dead spots, but she respected Zeb's decision and said nothing.

When lunch break arrived, Brash addressed his junior fellows.

"Highmost Cogg is taking a handful of the fellows, including myself, to a luncheon at Industry Manor. Because of this, you are all excused for the rest of the day. I encourage you to devote your time to the pursuit of knowledge." He made eye contact with Zeb for a little too long. Leilani's stomach twisted.

Most of the junior fellows left in a tight group, followed by their aides, also clumped together. Zeb stuck to Leilani's side, urging her towards the Observatory. "I want to see if they'll let me examine the telescope. No one ever uses it in the day, after all."

With most of the fellows at lunch, only a solitary librarian remained on duty. When Zeb asked, he unlocked the gate to the spiral staircase leading up to the viewing platform.

"Just don't turn any knobs–they have it set where they want it–and be careful not to fall," he cautioned.

He then returned to his desk, propped his feet up, and

stuck his nose back in his book.

The platform surrounding the telescope consisted of grated metal and hovered about a dozen feet above the floor of the library. The railing stood at chin height, and Leilani had to rise to her tiptoes to gaze over it. A table and chairs, the one where Cogg and Brash had met the day before, lay beneath her. She glanced out over the library. Two female junior fellows came through a door, shoulder to shoulder. One was Marce, the girl Zeb disliked from the Country House. Leilani ducked when they turned towards her location, not wanting to be caught staring.

She glanced at Zeb. The young Highmost was reading all the labels beneath the dozens of dials and switches on the telescope. Leilani pressed her finger to her lips and motioned downwards as the girls settled in the chairs below them.

"So there were no Strains at all?" the other girl, a blonde Leilani didn't recognize, asked. A chill cut through her. She focused on the conversation.

"None, Ves, *at all*," Marce said. "I ran around in circles looking for them for nearly ten minutes before they came back, but I swear I couldn't hear even a whisper."

Zeb nudged Leilani.

"One of the boys at dinner had a similar story. I thought he was just trying to scare me," Ves said. "So what did you do?"

"I told Cogg. I should've gone to my father instead. Highmost Cogg was furious, called me a liar and a fool and said if I told anyone, even my father, I'd never get another fellowship. I'm only telling you because . . . well, I had to tell someone. What if it happens again?"

"Maybe it was just your imagination. Besides, it is best not to make waves in your first year. You're right to keep silent. . ." Ves's voice dropped slightly, and Leilani shifted, trying to hear. The metal clasp on her messenger bag clanked against the metal railing, and the girls beneath looked up then hurried away.

Leilani dared to breathe again. The Strains began a tense rhythm, like pattering rain.

"So it isn't just us," Zebedy said. "I almost feel sorry for Marce."

Leilani clenched her fists. "Cogg will intimidate anyone who tries to speak up."

Zeb's shoulders hunched. "But if more people find the dead spots, he can't continue to suppress the knowledge. Someone will learn of them, someone he can't bully, maybe from a different manor, and someone will do something."

"But what if it is too late?" Leilani hit the metal railing. The clang echoed through the Observatory. The librarian turned around at his desk, looked up at them, and placed his finger to his lips.

The girls sat on the platform, Leilani rubbing her hand and Zeb staring at the telescope as if it might possibly save them.

"What if Cogg is behind the dead spots?" Leilani sank her voice to a whisper.

"Brash seemed to think he might be. He promised to look into it."

"But have you seen how Brash cowers before Cogg? What can he hope to achieve?"

Zeb's gaze dropped to her lap. Leilani glanced at the chronometer that sat beside the telescope's eyepiece.

"Cogg should be out of his office for a few more hours. What if we go there, pretending we don't know he is out, and have a look inside? Maybe we'll see something, a clue."

Zeb rolled her eyes. "This isn't a scavenger hunt. I doubt he just leaves 'clues' lying on his desk. Even if he does, his aide probably wouldn't let us in."

"Would it hurt to try?" Leilani frowned. "Aren't questions and investigation the very spirit of Research?"

Zeb bit her lip then stood. "All right, but let's go quickly."

Leilani scrambled to her feet, wondering how to tell Zeb she didn't know the way, only to have her friend stride out of the room with clear purpose. Without hesitation, Zebedy made her way down the stairs and through a series of turns into a hall somewhere behind the library.

Leilani hadn't explored this section of the manor. The doors they passed bore engraved plaques identifying the senior fellows who maintained those offices. At the end of the hall stood tall double doors of carved dark wood, one of which was propped open. Warm, natural light flooded through from two great windows which overlooked the canals and the gardens beyond. A heavy wooden desk, covered in stacks of papers, sat before the windows.

The girls stepped into the room and looked about. To their left lay a glass-doored cabinet filled with books, to their right, another pair of double doors. An open ledger sat upon the desk with a handwritten note.

The Highmost of Research is out today. Please leave your name and manor or address, and I will contact you to make an appointment at a later time.–Dalia Times, Aide to Highmost Cogg

"His aide is out too," Leilani breathed. "Is this his desk?"

"No, this is his aide's desk. His is through there." Zeb pointed towards the doors.

Leilani tried the silver-plated knob. "Locked, and Strain-proof I bet." As if in answer the Strains whistled shrilly then faded into twittering.

"It's for the best. We shouldn't be here anyway." Zeb put her hand on Leilani's shoulder. "Let's go."

Leilani rubbed the back of her neck, mindful of the pins in her bun. "Keep a look out for me. I want to try something." She took out a pin and stuck it in the lock.

Zeb's jaw dropped. "Leilani! Stop!"

Leilani shot her a scowl. "If you don't want to, fine, leave. I can do this on my own. I want to know what is going on with Cogg."

Leilani turned back to her lock picking. Zeb moaned, pulled

at her braid, and moved to the door. Instead of leaving, she stationed herself where she could watch the hall, occasionally casting glances at Leilani. Leilani's heart eased.

The lock snapped open after only a dozen or so clicks, faster than she'd dared to hope.

"Come on!" she hissed.

The girls darted into Cogg's office. His desk had an intricate motif of gears and wheels carved into the front. It lacked the piles of papers present on his aide's desk. The only things on display were an ornate pen stand, an inkwell, and a leather journal.

"We need to hurry." Zeb stood in the doorway, one hand clenched about her braid.

"Here, read this. I'll check the drawers." Leilani tossed the journal to Zeb who fumbled but managed to catch it against her thighs before it hit the floor. She glared at Leilani and opened the book.

"Dates, times, names, just a schedule. He certainly meets with Brash a lot, considering how little they like each other. That is strange. There are numbers after the dates and the letters G. C. What could that mean?"

Leilani paused midway through closing a drawer of seeming junk. "That's a merchant abbreviation for Gelian Coin. I've seen it on the receipts the Merchant Guild gives my father. Is Cogg paying Brash for something?"

"Brash could be paying Cogg." Zeb flipped through the journal.

"Why though? Are they large amounts?"

"A lot more than my allowance. Senior fellows don't make much more than juniors. They do it for the glory. If Brash is making payments to Cogg, he has to be giving him nearly everything."

Leilani yanked open the next drawer. A collection of broken markstone sticks rolled noisily from front to back. She rummaged through scraps of paper and a collection of snuff boxes. The third drawer held a collection of novels with titles that made her blush. She slammed that drawer shut.

She pulled open the fourth drawer and found it empty. Disappointed, she shut it again. A thought struck her. All the other drawers were full to bursting. This one didn't have so much as dust. She opened it again and pried at the bottom. It wouldn't budge.

"What are you doing?" Zeb asked.

"I think this is a false bottom, but it won't move," Leilani grunted.

"Here, let me." Zeb leaned over the desk and whispered. "Can you see the drawer?" The Strains hummed. "A latch? Really? Can you loosen it?"

Leilani heard a gentle click.

"There, you could've done that. Basic beggar magic." Zeb walked around the desk as Leilani raised the slat of wood. A stack of wrinkled, yellow papers lay beneath.

Leilani drew one out. She saw a diagram of doors and passages, laid out like the Botanical Garden maze, only about a hundred times more complicated. "It looks like a map."

"Yes. Those are the tunnels. These must be from when they were still used for travel. What a funny thing to hide. Anyway, it isn't as if the tunnels are a big secret." Zeb thumbed through several pages of yellowed maps.

A sheet of white caught Leilani's eyes. "This looks new. What is it?"

Zeb laid the paper on the desk. Leilani read, scrawled in bold letters across the top, ***Schematics, Strain Amplifier***. Beneath this was a sketch of a cone attached by a hose to a box. The drawing had a cut away revealing the complicated interior of gears and glass tubes.

"It kind of looks like Brash's miniature Strain detector." Leilani touched Zeb's shoulder.

Zeb shuddered. "That doesn't mean . . . we knew he was working on something called an amplifier for Cogg. Besides, he's right. This couldn't cause dead spots. These coils create energy with the Strains and focus it through here." She touched the cone. "The result would be a burst of power. I'm not sure how it would manifest, but these dials seem to play with the frequency. If the volume and reverberations increased . . ." Zeb's mouth clamped shut. The Strains died to a whimper.

Leilani rolled her eyes. "You realize when you talk like that, it's the equivalent to me randomly spouting Rynaran at you. I have no idea–"

"He's weaponizing the Strains!" Zeb shoved the paper back into the drawer and slammed it shut. She pulled her braid across her face and breathed into it. "We have to get out of here." Without waiting for Leilani, she ran from the room.

Leilani took a moment to put everything back as it had been and lock the door once more before following. She didn't catch up to Zeb, but took a guess and headed for their quarters.

Zeb sat reading a book when Leilani entered. She looked up, her eyes troubled.

"Brash shouldn't be working on something so dangerous. He should know better."

Leilani sat on the edge of her friend's bed. "That could be why Cogg is paying him. Greed can make people–"

"But Brash is all about discovery and knowledge, not money. He . . . he . . ."

"He may not be the man you think he is, or there may be another option. What exactly do these amplifiers do?"

Zeb let out a long breath and flipped back a few pages in her book to a picture of a box filled with the same sorts of gears and tubes as the schematic.

"Several decades ago, a Research fellow built this. He called it a 'Focus Box,' not an amplifier, but it essentially does the same thing. Fellow Verge found that by funneling the Strains through his device he could manipulate them. He'd adjust frequency and amplitude like he was directing them in a symphony. For a long while, he was the darling of all the manors, likely to be promoted to the Highmost Seat.

"Then something went horribly awry. Verge kept coaxing the Strains to extremes. He found how to make them break glass, influence plant growth, crack bricks in half, and temporarily numb the senses of everyone in the room. One day he accidentally *blinded* an assistant. People started to worry he had gone too far, but he wouldn't listen."

"But how did they stop him?" Leilani asked, her stomach tightening into a knot. Causing the Strains to harm others was the worst thing she could imagine doing to them or with them. The Strains fluttered like rustling leaves.

Zeb shrugged. "He stopped himself. Knocked his whole workshop down on top of his head and destroyed his device. Some said it was suicide. Anyway, after that, all the manors agreed to let his findings gather dust. For every potential benefit to his findings, there were a myriad of risks. Some fellows protested the decision to halt the research. You could do things with focused Strains. Things most Highmost couldn't imagine."

Leilani scratched the top of her head. "And this amplifier does the same things?"

"From what I can tell, it's very similar. The main difference is that cone attachment. I think you could use that to aim the Strains. There are benevolent uses for such a device. Cogg and Brash might mean to use it for good." Zeb unfolded her legs.

"Then why hide it?" Leilani took the book and gazed at the drawing.

"Because benevolent or malevolent, it's still illegal. If people knew Cogg continued Verge's work, he would lose his office, or worse."

Leilani examined the picture. It certainly looked like the schematics. The text underneath didn't say anything about such devices destroying the Strains, only increasing them.

"None of this explains the dead spots or why Cogg is paying Brash," Zeb echoed Leilani's thoughts. "Also, why the maps of the tunnels?"

Tunnels. Where have I heard or seen something about the tunnels? Vickers!

"Zeb, if something odd is going on in the tunnels, Vickers might know."

Zeb opened her eyes wider then squinted. "Would he help us, though?"

"He seemed friendly. Maybe he's changed. If we explain what is going on, he could understand how important it is."

Zeb rubbed the space between her eyes as if it hurt. "I guess it's our best chance. Let's go to Civics."

Chapter Fifteen

Vickers's office lay amongst a maze of storage rooms in the back of Civics Manor. This section of the manor had a barren, almost unfinished quality, as if the builders had slapped on a quick coat of gray paint and called it good. It seemed especially stark when compared to the grand front rooms with their marble pillars and gold embellishments.

"At least we'll have privacy," Leilani said at their third right, wondering if the clerk who had given them directions had been trying to get them lost.

"He can't be doing as well as I thought if they stuck him back here." Zeb gazed down the unlit hall. A thin line of light seeped under the door at the end.

Zeb stopped in front of the door but didn't reach for the knob. Leilani rolled her eyes and knocked.

"Come in," Vickers's voice came through the door.

Zeb shifted from foot to foot. Leilani opened the door and shoved her friend through.

Vickers sat behind his desk with his feet propped up. His glasses rested low on his nose, and he held a book in his hand. When he saw Zeb, he bolted upright and pushed the glasses back into place. His hand strayed to his hair then fell back to his side.

A smile crept over his face. "Zebedy, I . . . Hi."

She sniffed. "Could they have hidden your office any better?"

Leilani elbowed her but had to admit she'd been thinking something similar. It was a small room, and so crammed with bookshelves there was barely space for Vicker's desk and chair.

His smile faded. "I requested it. I like the quiet."

Leilani stepped around Zeb, and Vickers eyed her.

"Did you come here just to insult my office?"

"No, we need access to the tunnels," Zeb said.

Vickers raised his eyebrows. "Why?"

Zebedy's shoulders stiffened. "I'm not sure I can tell you."

Leilani nudged Zeb's arm and hissed in her ear. "We need his help. At least give him the abridged version."

Zeb gave an exaggerated sigh. "There is something strange going on at Research, and we think it may involve the tunnels."

"Why?" Vickers set his book down on the desk.

Leilani and Zeb exchanged a glance. They couldn't tell him about poking around in Cogg's office.

"We saw some maps of the tunnels during our investigation," Zeb said.

"That doesn't mean anything. Tunnel maps are public record. Anyone who wants to can request copies from the file room. Here." He took a rolled blueprint from under his chair, flattened it onto his desk, and weighed down the corners with his book, an inkwell, and two metal paperweights in the shape of howling wolves. "This is the entire system. Nothing strange about it, though you can easily get lost if you don't bring a light and a compass."

"Or you could just use the Strains," Zeb said.

"Sometimes I like to do things the hard way." Vickers shrugged. "Now, are you going to tell me what this is all about?"

Zeb's mouth clamped shut, but Leilani just wanted to get it over with. "Have you ever heard of places without the Strains?" she asked.

"You mean outside of Gelia? Of course. From what I've heard, they only exist here."

"No, I mean within Gelia, inside the manors."

Vickers squinted in obvious puzzlement. "No. Something like that would cause a panic. Most Highmost can't get dressed without the Strains."

Zeb stood up straighter. "Just because we choose not to doesn't mean we can't."

Vickers snorted. “I didn’t mean you specifically, but if the shoe fits. What have you heard?”

“It's more what we *don’t* hear.” Zeb’s shoulders relaxed, though her eyes remained hard. “We’ve found dead spots, places where the Strains disappear.”

Vickers frowned. “Have you shown anyone?”

“One fellow, but Highmost Cogg forbids us to talk about them.”

The Strains shrieked. Everyone winced.

“See!” Zeb said. “They want you to believe me.”

“I heard.” Vickers rubbed his ears.

Leilani fidgeted, wishing she could understand what they said.

Vickers sat down and touched the map. “And you were somehow in the tunnels when you found these 'spots?'”

“No . . .” Zeb drew out the syllable. “The spots are scattered all over Research.”

“I don't understand why you need access to the tunnels. They are restricted for a reason. Half are structurally unstable and many completely filled with rubble. Just getting the major ones safe for travel will take years, and our plan is simply to brace and block the side passages. You could get hurt, or worse, wandering around in there.”

Zeb's brows melted into a V. “So much for coming to you if I needed anything,” she scoffed.

He held up his hands. “Ask for something I can give.”

Leilani drew a deep breath. The two Highmost stared at each other as if she wasn’t even there.

“Vickers,” Leilani said, “is there any way at all we can get into the tunnels? Perhaps with a guide?”

He coiled the blueprints back into a tight roll. “I can take you down there, but not today. I’ll need to double check some things first, make sure the tunnels under Research are safe.”

Leilani nodded. “That could work, right, Zeb?”

“I suppose,” her friend answered.

Vickers stood. “I'll send for you when I get everything arranged.”

“I look forward to it,” Zeb said, not sounding like she meant it.

Both girls turned towards the door.

Vickers cleared his throat. “Leilani, do you mind if I speak to you for a moment, alone?”

Leilani frowned at Zeb.

Zeb eyed Vickers, then turned to Leilani and shrugged. “If you want to talk to him, I'll wait in the lobby.”

“I won't be long.”

She waited until Zeb had disappeared down the hall to face Vickers.

The young man grimaced. “She still hates me, doesn't she? After all these years, I thought there was a chance she would've let it go. You know her better than anyone. Is she all right? This 'dead spot' thing seems to have her shaken.”

Leilani bit her bottom lip. “The Strains are everything to Zeb. The first time she encountered a dead spot she nearly passed out.”

He rubbed the back of his neck, his mouth still twisted. “I would like to help her. She obviously doesn’t trust me.”

Leilani crossed her arms over her chest. “Trust has to be earned. Though apologizing for the trick you played on her would go a long way. She still bristles every time she thinks about you, and it is all because of one stupid, cruel prank.”

He opened his mouth, closed it again, then shook his head. “I never meant . . .” He exhaled a long breath. “Some things can’t be undone. Thank you for your time, Miss Leilani.” He slumped into his chair and stared at the blank wall beside his desk.

Leilani sniffed. “Highmost are so ridiculously stubborn.” Her fingers tickled the door knob, but she drew her hand back and stared at Vickers once more. “Look, in all fairness, I have only heard Zeb’s story and that was years after the event in question. Do you want to tell your side?"

He laughed, though his mouth stayed down-turned. "You're Common, aren't you, Leilani?"

She drew back, prepared to snap at him if his next statement was in any way derisive. "Yes."

"Do you have a large family?"

"No. My parents have three children including myself."

His eyes left the wall and met hers. "For Highmost that would be considered large. It is rare for us to have more than one child and infertility is a frequent complaint. My father's focus in the Healing Manor has always been reproductive health. He thinks the Strains do something to us, perhaps as a way of controlling our numbers. Even if only one parent is Highmost, the child will inherit the ability. If we were capable of reproducing at normal rates, we'd soon overwhelm the Common."

"I noticed the difference in family size. I just assumed it was because you married later." Leilani couldn't imagine what this conversation had to do with anything.

"I suppose you've heard the stories of Common women having Highmost children?" He drummed his fingers on the desktop.

"I've never known anyone who had it happen to them, but rumors of it happening, yes. That's why infants are tested at birth."

"It can't happen, though. At least one parent has to be Highmost for the child to be. If a Common couple has a Highmost baby, the reason is infidelity, not fate. That is also why it generally happens to unwed mothers and why it is so simple for us to swoop in and 'reassign' the infant to Highmost parents. We try to keep it hushed, but when a childless couple suddenly has a little one in their care, people take note. I knew I'd been reassigned by the time I was six."

Leilani's jaw dropped. "You're part Common?"

He nodded. "My father's status keeps people from talking

about it, plus I'm almost certain he's my biological parent. My birth mother worked as a nurse in the Healing Manor, under him. It would've been a simple matter for him to have his bastard assigned to him. Dess, his wife, loved me as her own, which is more than I can say about 'dear old dad.'" He snorted. "Legally, a reassigned child is forbidden contact with his birth mother. Mom . . . er, my adopted mom, that is, never let rules stand in the way of what she saw as right. When I started asking questions, she arranged for me to meet my . . . other mom. She'd smuggle me into the Botanical Gardens to see her a few times a month and the three of us would talk and play. That's where my birth mom told me that stupid story about the chickens."

Leilani allowed her face to soften. "So it wasn't a lie?"

"No. After my mom died, I wasn't able to meet with my birth mother any longer, so I lost both of them. My dad couldn't wait to ship me off to the Country House, and on free weekends, he left me to my own devices. I don't make friends easily. For the most part, I just don't care. A good book and a quiet room is my idea of paradise, but there is something special about Zebedy. The way the Strains sing when she walks into a room, that smile . . . even when we were kids, I wanted to be with her. I felt safe telling her things, like that story."

Leilani nodded. "She has a way of getting people to talk. There's something disarming about her."

"I think it is how open she is. She told me her life story the first day we met, no guile, just a big smile and complete honesty. Made me . . ." He fell silent and rubbed his forehead.

"Why didn't you say something?" Leilani prodded.

"When the whole class turned on her, I should've. I froze, though. Admitting that I knew my birth mom would've caused a scandal. My mom made it clear I could never tell anyone." He glanced at the door then back down at the desk. "Afterward, well, our rivalry was fun. I thought maybe I could work with that, but now all she wants to do is fight with me."

Leilani stepped closer to him, something yielding inside her. “You like her a lot, don’t you?”

He laughed. “Does it show?”

“You know, telling her what you just told me would go a long way towards improving her opinion of you.”

He lowered his eyes. “People like me don’t end up with people like her. She’s right about me in a lot of ways. I like to be alone. I prefer facts to feelings, and that’s just who I am. If she doesn’t like that, she won’t like me. Plus I'm nearly impossible to live with.”

Leilani laughed. “You don't seem that difficult to me.”

“You should ask my aide about that,” he said, rolling his eyes.

Leilani paused. “I've never met your aide.”

“He quit three weeks ago. Told me my expectations were impossibly high, and it drove him crazy that I kept redoing his work because it wasn't 'up to snuff.' After he left, I realized I prefer to work alone.” He cleared his throat. “You’d better go catch up with her. I will see you when I get the tour arranged.”

Chapter Sixteen

Zeb waited at the end of the hall. She eyed Leilani. "What did he want?"

Leilani shrugged. "He's worried about you. Wanted to know if you were all right."

Zeb sniffed. "He probably thinks I'm going mad. I should've known he wouldn't understand."

Leilani winced. *Poor Vickers.*

Zeb led the way out of the maze of passages, consulting the Strains if she couldn't remember a turn. "At least he agreed to a guided tour. Let's get back to Research. Maybe Brash will have found something."

I doubt it, Leilani thought, but said nothing.

The girls left Civics through a side door. The wind picked up, and they huddled together against it as they walked. Leilani rubbed her arms, wishing for a coat.

"Here." Zeb whistled, and the Strains swirled about them, tinkling like chimes. The air thickened and warmed.

"Is there anything you can't use the Strains for?" Leilani laughed.

Zeb lowered her gaze. "Making people like me. I've never been able to figure that out."

Leilani patted her friend's back. "Everybody worth bothering about already likes you."

"You like me, and that's enough. I shouldn't bother about Vicky. He's always seen me as silly and gullible, and that isn't going to change."

Leilani opened her mouth then shut it again. If Vickers wouldn't speak for himself, it was none of her business. Maybe when things calmed down, she'd try and introduce the idea of reconciliation.

The girls continued on, hand in hand.

The gate to Research Manor came into view. Leilani squinted at the dark uniformed figures milling about the entrance.

"Are those guards?" she asked.

Zeb placed her hand above her eyes. "They are. What are they doing out here?"

They drew closer. Another pair approached from the direction of the Observatory. Leilani recognized Mistress Straight and her aide. The aide carried a large clipboard. One of the guards, who Leilani now identified as Captain Goodly, greeted them.

"Our current head count is short five, three juniors, an aide, and Fellow Brash. I found the aides of two of the missing juniors, and they thought they might've gone to the Gardens together." Straight glanced up. "Oh wait, here's two now. You're Junior Fellow Brightly, are you not? And you're her aide?"

The girls nodded. Straight's aide marked something on his clipboard.

Leilani and Zeb exchanged a worried glance.

Oh Strains, what if someone saw us in Cogg's office? Are we going to be arrested? Leilani tried to keep her face placid, but her stomach flopped.

Straight's eyebrows formed a neat V. "Where have you ladies been?"

"We were visiting a friend at Civics Manor," Leilani said, knowing Zeb might consider that a lie. Zeb was awful at lying.

"Can they verify that?" Straight's eyes narrowed.

"I suppose, but why?" Zeb asked.

Straight rubbed her hands together. "I hate treating my fellows as suspects, but nothing like this has happened before. Strains, what a nightmare!"

"That still leaves three unaccounted for," Goodly said. "Do you want me to send a man to the Gardens?"

Straight shook her head. “It is ridiculous to assume the culprit is a member of Research. The attacker could’ve sneaked in and out. I won’t believe one of my fellows did something like this.”

The word “attacker” struck Leilani in the breastbone, and she gaped. She glanced at Zeb.

The color drained from Zeb's face, leaving her already pale skin practically blue. “What happened?” She pulled at her braid.

“You’ll hear soon enough, hopefully when we’ve found out what really happened. Go to your rooms for now. If you can prove you were out of the manor at the time, you won’t even need to be tested.”

The girls entered the Observatory. The first hall they passed, which led to the library, had been roped off, and a guard stood in the gap. Relief swept over Leilani when she saw him, and she rushed to his side. He grinned at her, then grew grave again.

“Brick, thank the Maker! What is going on?”

Brick scratched the top of his head. He drew a finger across his neck in a slashing motion. Leilani glanced at Zebedy.

“Well, that’s clear, if crude,” Zeb said. “Someone was killed?”

He nodded.

“Killed?” Leilani's throat seized up. She hadn't heard of a murder in Gelia in her lifetime–accidents, occasionally, but murder, never. In between the guards and the Strains, it just never happened. She forced her tongue to move again. “That explains all the extra guards and Mistress Straight’s headcount. What do you think she meant by ‘tested,’ Zeb?”

“A Strains test, most likely. If someone killed someone else, they’d lose the Strains, so anyone who can still use them is ruled out as a killer.” Zeb's voice shook as she spoke. “The only way a Strains test wouldn't work would be if the killer was already known to be unable to hear the Strains, like some of the guards.”

Leilani shot her a glare, and Zeb quailed back. Fortunately, Brick had resumed his post, looking up and down the hallway, and had not been in a position to see Zeb's lips.

Zeb wrung her hands. "Who could've done something like this? Oh! And to whom? Who died?"

Leilani fished her notepad from her bag and tapped Brick on the shoulder. She spoke as she wrote. "Who died? Do you know?"

He nodded then made a circular motion as if turning a crank.

"Wheel? Circle? Pulley?" Leilani guessed, trying to write the names as fast as she could think them up.

"Oh!" Zeb's mouth fell open. She snatched the notebook from Leilani and scratched out four letters. "Cogg? Highmost Cogg?"

The Strains chirped like crickets.

"I'm afraid so." The voice from behind made Leilani jump. She whirled to face Brash. The fellow wore a heavy black cloak and gloves. "Captain Goodly found me on my walk and informed me of Cogg's death." He stepped towards Brick and raised his hands. His fingers flashed as blindingly as Brick's did when signing. Brick raised his eyebrows and responded in kind.

"You know his language?" Leilani asked.

"A sufficient amount of it." A smile played at the corners of Brash's mouth before he grew grave again.

Leilani's suspicions eased . . . slightly.

"Apparently a junior found his body, still warm, less than an hour ago. Do I have my details right?" He raised his palms upward towards Brick, who nodded. "How was he killed?"

Brick slapped himself on the back of the head.

"Bludgeoned? Sounds more like an act of passion than planning. Did they find a weapon?"

Brick shook his head.

Brash cleared his throat. "Miss Brightly, Aide Weaver, may we speak in private?"

Leilani hesitated, but Zeb hurried after him. With a sigh and a wave to Brick, Leilani followed.

Brash led the girls around the corner, away from Brick. "If this somehow involves your dead spots, then things are more dangerous than I had thought. You must promise not to resume your investigations. If someone died because of this, you need to stay out of the whole thing."

"But with Cogg no longer forbidding it, why can't we tell people?" Zeb shifted from foot to foot. "People need to know."

Brash shook his head. "There is too much risk. In a few days, the senior fellows will elect a new Highmost for Research. When that is settled, I will speak to them about this. Until then, you must promise not to endanger yourselves." He reached out and clasped Zeb's hand. "You have a promising future. You must protect that, Miss Brightly." His voice took on a simpering tone. "Promise me you won't put yourself in danger investigating this."

"I promise!" Zeb burst out.

Leilani's stomach twisted. "Zeb, but . . ."

"He'll take care of it, Leilani. We can trust him."

Leilani stared at Fellow Brash, trying to gaze into his soul.

Come on, Strains. Give me a sign.

The rhythms about her didn't change.

The fellow smiled a faint smile. He reached into his pocket and pulled out a watch on a chain. "Look, if I had been involved in Cogg's death, I wouldn't be able to do this. Up now!" The timepiece floated into the air. It hovered for a moment before falling into his open hand.

Leilani hesitated. Maybe his hand hadn't struck the blow, but he could be tangentially involved. She needed to get away from him.

"I promise not to do anything stupid," she said.

He nodded. "That's always a good plan. Excuse me, girls."

Leilani watched him disappear back down the hall. A moment later Brick stepped out of the side passage he had been guarding to allow two men carrying a sheet-draped stretcher by. Leilani shuddered.

Zeb touched Leilani's shoulder, her fingers quivering. "Let's get ready for dinner. I don't want to be out here right now. I'm relieved Brash is taking over if people are going to start dying. This is just too dangerous, and I wasn't looking forward to stumbling around in the dark with Vickers, anyway."

"We can't just give up," Leilani said.

Zeb pulled away as if struck. "We have to. We promised."

"You promised. I just said I wouldn't do anything stupid, and trusting someone we barely know with something this important is the definition of stupid."

Zeb unplaited her braid and ran her fingers through the wavy strands. "But I promised, and what do you mean, 'barely know'? I've known him as long as you've known that guard you've been following around."

Leilani sighed. "Zeb, I won't make you do anything you don't want to do, but this is important. What if the dead spots spread? What if someone does weaponize the Strains? We know Brash was helping Cogg with the Amplifiers. How can we trust him?"

"I trust him. Isn't that enough for you?" Zeb rubbed her arms. The Strains gave a low, melancholy moan.

Leilani's chest tightened. "I trust Brick. Is that enough for you?"

Zeb fell silent, and the girls walked back to their room accompanied by the uneasy dirge of the Strains.

Chapter Seventeen

In their room that evening, Zeb penned a dismissive note to Vickers, canceling their appointment.

"He'll think you are avoiding him," Leilani pointed out.

"He won't be completely wrong, and I doubt he cares." Zeb sniffed. "Cross-Manor . . . friendships rarely work. I need to pursue relationships within Research, not Civics."

"I'll take it down to the courier's office, if you want," Leilani said as Zeb pressed her starburst seal into the red wax.

"Would you? I want to get some reading done. With all this clandestine nonsense, I'm falling behind."

"Classes will probably be canceled tomorrow because of Cogg's death, anyway," Leilani pointed out.

Zeb winced and rubbed her arms. "All the more reason to read. I need something to keep my mind off what happened today."

As soon as the door to their room shut behind her, Leilani took a markstone stick out of her bag and scrawled, *Just tell her the truth–Leilani* on the outside of the envelope. Zeb could use an anchor. Vickers might have the appropriate weight.

Leilani hurried through the hushed halls. She passed several guards where they wouldn't normally be and saw few Highmost. The ones she did encounter averted their eyes and moved quickly, as if they were suspects who, in turn, suspected everyone else. Even the Strains seemed depressed, humming in a minor key with little rhythm.

The courier's office was closed for the night, but she slipped the message through the slot in the door, confident it would be delivered first thing in the morning.

In spite of the Strains' apparent lethargy, she drew them about her like a blanket. "I think you like Brick, don't you? And you like Zeb a lot. I can't understand how she can leave you in the hands of Brash. What do you think of Brash?"

The Strains fell silent.

She stumbled, catching herself on the wall. Her insides twisted, but she forced herself forward into the empty heart of the dead spot. Her steps rang out like hammer strokes. She pushed through the void, along the hallway, past several side passages. She had never had one stretch on for so long. Up ahead lay the turn towards the kitchen. Brick could be there. The dinner hour had just ended, and the guards ate later than the Highmost.

Longing for his company, she headed in that direction. Warm relief swept over her when the Strains rose to meet her. However, their tones remained subdued. She paused to absorb them, drawing strength from their presence.

The smell of roast chicken wafted through the passage. Leilani followed her nose to the kitchen. The sounds of human merriment, splashing water, and clanking dishes overwhelmed the sickly Strains.

To her relief, several guards, including Brick, lingered about their table. A stack of dirty plates teetered beside them, waiting for a dishwasher to whisk them away. Brick sat with one leg bent beneath him, a block of wood and knife in hand. Two older guards appeared to watch his every move as he turned the block over, shaving off small strips here and large chunks there.

When Leilani approached, Brick waved the knife in greeting. The other guards chuckled and moved away, allowing Leilani to sit beside him.

"What are you making?"

He brushed his fingers across both his cheeks then made a clawing motion.

She mirrored his movements. "A cat?"

He smiled and resumed carving. His calloused hands seemed to glide over the rough wood as the chips fell. The scratching of the knife tickled her ears, and she drew closer to him, inhaling the smell of the pine. The blade caught on a knot with a snap, and he wiggled it until it broke free. All other noises faded as she concentrated on his movements. The piece formed within his hands as the scraps peeled away, revealing the sleek, rounded form of a stretching feline. She sighed contentedly.

He shifted the knife into his other hand and reached out and touched her cheek. She gazed up at him. Leaning towards her, he formed his hand into a c-shape, facing his chest, then turned it outward with a shrugging motion.

She shook her head. "Sorry, that one doesn't . . . I don't know what you mean."

He repeated the sign, then stroked her face again, raising his eyebrows in a clear question.

"Oh, I'm fine. It has just been a long day."

He nodded and resumed carving.

Leilani reached for Brick's arm but drew her hand back. She wanted to touch him but had no idea how. Their hand holding had been such a distinct pleasure, but with his fingers hard at work on his carving, it didn't seem practical.

She closed her eyes and imagined they were alone. She would drape herself over his shoulders like a cape and hide her face in the top of his head. What would his hair smell like? Would he like that or would he think it strange?

Her eyes jerked open when his fingers circled her wrist. She blushed at his peering gaze. He opened his mouth in an o and patted his lips with his hand, clearly mimicking a yawn.

"No, I'm not tired."

He reached into his pocket and pulled out a notepad and a stub of a markstone stick.

She laughed as she took it and began to write.

Everything in my life has changed over the last few days, and it feels like I'm just along for the ride. I don't like that. I like to make choices, not have them made for me. Plus with what happened to Cogg, I just feel strange. I didn't really know him, but I don't think I've ever spoken to someone and had

them dead the next day.

Brick read the note then tucked the pad back into his pocket. Standing, he moved to sit behind her on the bench. His arms came about her waist, and he slipped his blade into her hand. Shivers ran up her arm when his skin touched hers. She blushed. He held out the cat carving.

"Oh no, I'll ruin it. You've done such a good job so far. . ." Realizing he couldn't see her lips from his new position, she stopped. She turned her head, and their noses brushed. She pushed the statuette back at him and used the sign, circling her hand over her smiling face. "Beautiful. Your work is beautiful. I don't want to ruin it."

He shook his head and laid his hand across the back of hers.

She sighed. "All right, but I warned you."

She carefully drew the knife across the wood, towards herself. Brick shook his head, carefully pried open her fingers, and turned the blade around. He guided her hand away from her body. A thin curl of pine fell from the work, and she grinned. Examining the piece, she shaved off another line. The Strains sang in her ears, like humming human voices, and she remembered how her father used them to guide his threads. Perhaps something similar could be accomplished with wood.

She hummed along, coaxing the Strains around her knife. They nudged her in the same direction as Brick's gentle leading, helping her to steady her hand and find the natural grain of the wood. Shavings piled in her lap.

The tension between her shoulders melted away. She hadn't even realized she'd been carrying so much. His breath warmed the back of her neck. Her movements slowed then stopped altogether. The cat remained only half done, but Brick didn't seem to care, and she certainly didn't. His chin rubbed against the top of her head, and her muscles turned to jelly against him.

After several minutes, he withdrew his arms and stood.

She gazed up at him. He tapped his wrist cuffs then pointed to the door with a grimace.

"You have to go back to work?" she asked, disappointed, but proud she had understood him. He nodded. Standing, she passed him his knife and placed the unfinished statue on the table. "Maybe I can see you tomorrow? I want to see you."

He grinned, waved, and left, collecting his saber and pistol from a rack by the door.

She lingered in the kitchen. She didn't feel like going back to her quarters yet. Perhaps she'd see if the library was still roped off. Slipping into the empty hall, she addressed the Strains. "If only you talked to me the way you talked to Zeb. You could tell me what to do next. Of course, you don't seem to know everything. If you did, couldn't you just tell us who killed Cogg and what is causing the dead spots?"

The Strains murmured musically, perhaps in answer. A strand of hair had worked its way out of her bun, so she tucked it behind her ear.

"You do seem to tell Zeb things, and sometimes I swear you are guiding me. Perhaps you really don't know the answers here, though." She stopped and leaned against the wall, listening as the Strains filled the otherwise silent space. What did it mean that they couldn't know? Could the force causing the dead spots be blinding the Strains? Or perhaps the Strains didn't see the way people did at all. Perhaps they were blind even as Brick was deaf. After all, Brick functioned perfectly well without working ears. Why would the Strains need eyes?

"Can you see me?" she whispered.

As if in response, she heard shuffling, not the Strains, but the solid sound of soft shoes on tile floors. The Strains gave a quivering chirp then fell silent.

Leilani bolted from the wall. Whoever approached would feel the dead spot. They'd be another witness. The footsteps grew closer, and she watched as a cloaked figure, wrapped from head to toe in bulky cloth, emerged from a side hall. He stood only feet away, his back was to her. He continued walking, and she gaped. Was he Wordless? How was he not reacting to the lack of Strains?

As the man disappeared down the hall, the Strains returned. Her heart shuddered. She pursued the cloaked man, and when she drew near him the Strains died again.

She kept close to the wall, though the man never looked behind him. He kept to darkened side halls. Reaching the gate to the tunnels, he stopped and drew a key from his cloak. He laid something on the ground, a glinting, silver cylinder, perhaps a foot high.

Hiding in an alcove, she watched as he unlocked the gate, entered, and locked it again behind himself. A moment later the Strains flooded the area, chirping like caged birds suddenly free.

Leilani swallowed. The man, whoever he was, held the answer, the missing piece.

"Please be here when I get back," she whispered.

The Strains gave a plaintive wail, but Leilani ignored them, slipped a pin from her hair, and hurried to the gate.

Chapter Eighteen

As the lock fell open in her hand, the Strains danced around her with the hectic energy of a child pounding on a toy piano. Leilani hesitated. The shadowy candlelight from the hall only reached as far as the third step. Below that lay bottomless darkness. She wished she knew Zeb's light tricks. She placed her hand on the wall and guided herself into the tunnel, closing her eyes to help them adjust.

She opened her eyes at the bottom of the stairs, and it was as if they had remained shut.

This won't do.

She glanced about. Behind her the light from the upper level beckoned. She fumbled about in her bag. Perhaps Zeb had included something useful in this hodgepodge. Her eye caught a glow, so faint she thought it imagined. Her fingers brushed over it and felt cool, solid glass. She drew out a small canister, the length of her longest finger. Inside bubbled a phosphorescent liquid. When her hand moved the tube, it grew brighter, allowing her a three step circle of light. Leilani started forward, shaking the light source every few feet to keep it shining.

Leilani wondered how Zeb used the Strains for finding her way out of the garden maze. Was it a Highmost trick or something she could learn? Whatever it was, it hadn't prevented Zeb from getting lost on multiple occasions.

She came to the first fork. The path broke into three tunnels before her.

"So Strains, which way did he go?"

The Strains whistled.

"Well, I can guess, or turn back or . . ." She knelt down and examined the floor, tracing it with the Strains for even the slightest markings in the dust. The first two branches hadn't been disturbed, but the Strains dipped into slight divots in the third, increasing the depth of the marks so they were easily visible for Leilani. She smiled.

Sometimes beggar magic simply meant Common sense.

She shuffled her feet as she walked, hoping to leave tracks she could follow back. The vague stories haunted her, tales of folk becoming lost and wandering until starvation and madness took them. She wasn't supposed to be in this place. No one would look for her here. She had to be able to find her way out.

Several turns and forks and appeals to the Strains later, the tunnel dead-ended in front of a hole in the floor. She stopped. The opening had a smooth brick casing, like a well, and a rusty metal ladder stuck out of it. Where could it go? Nothing lay beneath the tunnels.

She hid her light canister in her cloak and waited for her eyes to adjust to the darkness. The man couldn't be traveling blind, and she couldn't be far behind him. Perhaps . . . She leaned over the edge. Yes, a weak illumination warmed the bottom of the ladder. Placing her light source in her pocket, she descended. The pitted metal of the ladder caught on her skin.

The last several steps hung in mid-air, stopping two or three feet from the ground. She paused to listen. Below her lay a packed earth floor, bathed in faint light. She took a deep breath, prayed the man wouldn't be waiting for her, and dropped the last few feet. She landed in a crouch.

Finding herself facing a rounded brick wall, she turned as she stood and gazed into a forest of smooth, stone columns. Shadows lay like dark stripes upon the floor, and she stepped into one of these to shield herself. A clicking, hissing sound filled the air. Not the Strains, but something mechanical. She could make out the far wall, and estimated the room to be about the size of the library in the manor above. In the center lay an open space, and there stood the hooded man, light emanating from a lantern in his hand. Around him stood four man-high cylinders with multiple funnels sticking out of the sides. Dials whirred next to what appeared to be a shut off or pressure release valve.

She moved closer. Were they steam boilers? Storage tanks? Three columns away, she paused. The Strains whispered thinly, not quite gone but dying . . . and suffering. They emitted a constant, wordless wail, like a grease-less wheel grinding down a rusty track, growing fainter in the distance.

Her jaw clenched, and her fingers tightened into fists. *It's sucking the life from them. They need to break free.*

The funnel extensions aimed upward, towards the manor above. Could they be drawing the Strains over such a distance? Causing the dead spots?

She shoved back her urge to rush forward and dismantle the machines. Who knew what the stranger would do if he caught her?

He removed a canister, about the size of a wine bottle, and attached it to a rubber hose coming off one of the larger cylinders. Leilani needed to bring someone here, to show them, to stop *him*. She backed away, but before she could hide behind the next column, he looked up.

The man's body stiffened. His hood hid his eyes, but she knew he had seen her. He pulled the canister from the hose and flung it at her as she turned to run. The bottle impacted against the floor several columns away, and a cracking sound, like a giant swinging a whip, exploded around her. A wave of cacophonous sound knocked Leilani from her feet. Her vision swam, and her ears rang.

The Strains screamed.

A dozen agonized voices, each with a different tone, overwhelmed her then dissipated. Aching silence grabbed at her, and in spite of her pain and disorientation, she forced herself to her feet.

She clambered up the ladder and pulled her body into the darkened tunnel. She fished her light source from her pocket.

Follow the steps. Fast. Don't look back. Don't stop. Don't think.

Her chest rose and fell painfully, and her legs shook, but she pushed onward, as fast as her legs could carry her. The tunnels seemed to stretch on even longer than they had on her way down. She gulped in breaths.

The sound of dying Strains, so loud and visceral, ached in her ears. She wanted to hear their music again, to cleanse their keening from her mind. Tears blinded her.

She had always known the Strains lived. Living things could suffer. Living things could die. Worse, though, they had been turned into weapons. If that blast had landed closer, Leilani had no doubt she would've been injured or killed. Those Strains had been forced to violate their very nature, and it had destroyed them.

She dared not glance behind her. Up ahead torchlight flared, beckoning. She made the stairs and climbed them on all fours. Reaching the closed gate, she collapsed to her knees, her light hitting the floor. She pushed against the gate.

It was locked. Her eyes adjusted. On the other side, holding lanterns, stood Captain Goodly and Mistress Straight. Behind them cowered Brash's aide, Kasan Morgan.

"Well," Mistress Straight said coldly. "You'd better have a good reason for being in there."

Chapter Nineteen

Leilani trembled as Goodly drew the key from his pocket and opened the gate. The shrieks of the dying Strains tainted the music of the living. They danced in her head like demons in a nightmare. Unable to bear the memory a moment longer, she burst into tears.

"Crying won't help you," Straight snapped. "When Mr. Morgan told me he'd found the tunnel doors unlocked, I had hoped it was a simple oversight, but when Goodly discovered the lock had been picked . . ." Leilani raised her face and Straight stiffened. "You are an *aide*, not a burglar. Where did you learn to pick locks?"

Leilani gasped for breath. She had to tell them about the man, the Strains, everything! She didn't know where to start.

"Leilani!" Zeb rushed to them. "When you didn't come back, I got worried. Thank the Strains." She glanced at Goodly and Straight. "What's going on?"

"Miss Brightly, your aide took an unauthorized tour of a restricted area. Did you know anything about it?"

Zeb started to shake her head then stopped. Her mouth opened and closed, and for a moment Leilani thought she would blurt out everything. Then Zeb said, "I didn't know she was in the tunnels."

Leilani's pulse throbbed in her ears and throat. The Strains called to her, but she couldn't get a grasp on them. They were discordant, jarring, distant. She wanted to draw them closer and listen to them, but the memory of their dying brethren kept her from reaching out.

"Why were you in the tunnels?" Goodly stepped forward and pulled Leilani from her knees. Her legs shook, but he kept both hands on her shoulders. She leaned into him and managed not to fall.

"There's a man in the tunnels. I followed him." She gulped air. "He's killing the Strains."

Zeb went white, but the other faces ranged from confused to enraged. Goodly looked to Straight who scowled.

"Nonsense," she said. "Killing the Strains? Impossible. You can hear them all about us. If you are going to lie, girl, do it intelligently. What are you hiding?"

"Nothing . . . I . . . Zeb?"

Her friend's mouth clamped shut.

"Maybe she killed Cogg and that's why she's slinking around," Kasan piped up. All eyes turned towards the usually timid aide.

Straight's eyebrows shot up then pinched together. "She wasn't Strain tested."

"You said she had an alibi, Mistress." Goodly's fingers tightened into Leilani's shoulder, not painfully but firmly enough that she pulled herself out of her slouch.

"I haven't had a chance to verify that. Show us, girl. Use the Strains."

Leilani's head swam, and the world went gray around the edges. Cold sweat broke out across her forehead. Goodly squeezed harder.

Use the Strains? Now?

She tried to sing to them, but could only wheeze.

Pull yourself together. You can do this.

She opened her mouth, but before she could speak, the light vial floated up from the ground, and hovered before her eyes.

Mistress Straight nodded. Leilani swallowed her shock, reached for, and grabbed the light, her breath still ragged.

Straight sniffed. "Well, you may be a liar, but at least you aren't a murderer. Miss Brightly, your choice of aides was poor, but Fellow Brash thinks highly of you and I of him. For his sake, I will take you at your word. If you had nothing to do with this, dismiss your aide and return to your room. A new aide will be assigned to you in the morning."

Zeb stumbled back as if struck. "But she didn't hurt anybody. You saw her use the Strains . . ."

"The manors are held together by rules, Miss Brightly." Straight's cold eyes flickered. "If your aide has no respect for such things, it makes me doubt your commitment to the manors. You remember that I oversee all junior fellowships? Do you wish your appointment to be revoked?"

"No, Mistress Straight," Zeb said, her voice cracking. "But . . . even Brash has felt the dead spots. He can vouch for her, for us! Please, let me see Brash. He can clear this all up."

"I will *not* involve Fellow Brash in this foolishness. You will be lucky if he still considers you worthy of studying beneath him after tonight."

Goodly touched Straight's shoulder. "Mistress, it will only take about an hour to investigate the tunnels. If there is some truth to what the girls say about the Strains–"

"Of all the people here, Captain, you are the least qualified to discuss the Strains." Straight turned her nose up at Goodly.

The captain's face turned red, and Leilani longed to slap Straight on his behalf.

Straight focused on Zeb once more. "As for you, you have a choice. You can send your aide out of this manor or you can go with her, carrying a permanent mark on your record."

Zeb quivered and shook and opened and shut her mouth like a fish gasping for water.

"Well?" Straight tapped her foot.

Leilani stared into Zeb's watery eyes.

Zeb dropped her gaze. "Leilani . . . you . . . you can't be my aide any more."

An icicle plunged through Leilani's heart.

Straight waved her hand at the captain. "Captain Goodly, escort this girl to collect her belongings then see her out of the manor. Mr. Morgan, thank you for alerting us to the breach. I will make sure Fellow Brash knows of your initiative."

Straight and Kasan disappeared down the hall.

"Come," Goodly said. "Let's go get your things."

Goodly hung back a few steps, perhaps so that Leilani could unashamedly cry as they walked. Zeb caught up to her.

"I didn't want to do that, but if she questioned my involvement, I could lose my fellowship. What were you thinking?" Zeb hissed.

"Why didn't you tell her about the dead spots?" Leilani snarled through gritted teeth.

Zeb's mouth dropped open. "Because I swore to let Brash take care of it. I promised. You should've waited."

"Someone's killing the Strains, and you're doing nothing. If you had backed my story, they might have caught him, you coward." She shoved Zeb. "How could you stay silent?"

Zeb grabbed her arm. "I lied for you. I fooled the Strains test for you. You made me have to *lie,* Leilani." She shook Leilani, her face reddening.

Leilani had wondered if Zeb had been behind the floating vial. "I could've done it myself. I didn't need you."

"Yes, you do. I wanted this to be perfect. It has all fallen apart because you won't listen. Why won't you listen?" Zeb trembled like a drenched kitten. "You never believe me. You think I'm silly and weak, but I'm not. I know how manor politics works. I know how to trust. Brash said he would handle it. Why couldn't you take our word? No, instead, you are off gallivanting with dumb as a Brick."

Leilani shoved Zeb as hard as she could. The taller girl wobbled and fell onto her rump. She stared up at Leilani. Leilani blinked back at her, too angry to speak.

Zeb shrieked, and the Strains grabbed Leilani by the hair and tugged until the skin of her scalp raised off her skull. Leilani screamed and kicked out at Zeb.

The Strains clashed like cymbals, setting her off balance, and she covered her ears.

Zeb buried her face in her knees. "They don't like this. This is so wrong. Leilani, I know you can't understand them, but me, you have to. . ."

"Shut up!" Leilani shrieked. "I understand them better than you. I'm not the one letting them die!"

Goodly pushed his way between them. Zeb stood, rubbing her lower back, her eyes teary. Leilani's eyes stung, but she forced a glare. She'd cried enough for one day.

"Why are we even friends?" Leilani reached up and claimed the hair pins dangling from her uncoiled bun. "You are the most shallow, self-centered baby I have ever met."

Zeb's shoulders slumped. "No, I'm not. You don't mean that."

Leilani turned away. "I need to get my stuff."

Zeb did not follow Leilani and Goodly. Leilani made a point of not looking back until they reached the room.

Leilani's belongings easily fit into a small satchel. Goodly waited outside while she changed out of her uniform coat into the one Common outfit she'd brought with her, a plain gray frock and knee high boots.The majority of her messenger bag's contents had been gifts from Zeb. She considered returning them, but she'd been through enough. Zeb owed her a few markstone sticks and light tubes.

Leilani stuffed her clothes in on top of the miscellany. She exhaled long breaths through pursed lips, wishing the air could come out of her superheated ears as well. Losing her fellowship concerned Zeb more than the truth, than the Strains, than Leilani!

In spite of her determination not to cry, she sniffled. She had nothing: no plans, no future. It had been foolish to tie her fate to a Highmost, to Zeb. Leilani might as well have anchored herself to a butterfly.

Goodly knocked at the door. She shoved her hairbrush and box of pins into her pack and went out to meet him.

They walked in silence to the gates. He looked up and

down the darkened street. The circles of lamplight lay in both directions like a string of golden pearls. Mist drifted by the lamps, and the cold caused Leilani's nose to run once more.

"Do you have a place to stay in the Manor District?" he asked.

Leilani shook her head. "My family is in the Trade District."

His frown deepened. "That is a long walk." He reached up and unfastened his waist-length cloak. "Go to the Leisure District. Don't stop upon the way. Look for guards and keep to the lights. Gelia City is a different place at night. Other than my brethren, no good folk are about. The Cathedral will give you a cot. They are usually reserved for the homeless, but you will not be turned away." He draped his cape over her shoulders. "I must return to my post now. Take care, Miss Leilani."

She watched him disappear into the manor then stepped forward into the cold, empty night.

Chapter Twenty

Leilani walked. She disappeared between the lights then grew into a giant when she stepped into their circles and her shadow lengthened.

Presumably guards patrolled the districts, but she reached the first bridge having seen no one. Hearing a cough from a darkened alley, she quickened her pace.

Her boots clicked over the stone surface of the bridge. She reached the other side and paused for breath. The smell of grass, more intense for the darkness and the chill, filled her nose. She tightened Goodly's cloak about her. Finally, she'd reached the Leisure District. Sanctuary lay nearby.

The Strains purred to her, finally recovered from the trauma in the tunnels. She drew on them for courage. Maybe she could still save them. Someone somewhere would listen. They had to. Vickers, perhaps, or even other Common. She would find someone who would listen, but not now. Now she just needed to get somewhere safe.

The sound of footfalls rapping on the bridge behind her caused her to cringe. She glanced back. Three long shadows stretched like fingers towards her. Not guards, guards traveled in pairs.

No good folk are about.

The trees and hedges of the Leisure District lacked the illumination of the Manor District. Her feet crunched loudly on the gravel path, so she stepped off onto the grass.

"Hey! You!"

She ducked her head and pressed onward, as if she hadn't heard.

"You crossed our bridge. You must pay our toll." The young voice had a rowdy tone. She ran, breaking through the hedge lining the path. Her cloak snagged on a twig, and she let it fall.

"Get back here!" a second youth yelled.

Branches cracked and snapped behind her, and someone grabbed her by the shoulder. He pulled her back. His fingers glowed with the Strains. She squinted as the light fell across her face. A teen, with a beard like bread mold on his pale face, grinned.

"It's a girl!" He chortled. His friends gathered around, a dark-eyed youth in a cap and a pock-marked, curly haired boy, scarcely Leilani's age by his face. The pocked boy grabbed her chin. She wrenched away.

"Let me go!" she squeaked. The Strains trilled shrilly. The capped youth snatched her bag. He dumped her possessions to the ground, pawing over them with blazing fingers. At least two of these boys were Highmost then. "Ah, clothes and books. Nothing valuable."

"That's all right." Mold-beard leaned towards her face. "Perhaps she can find other ways to pay."

Leilani stiffened, her mind racing. The Strains would not kill, even for her, but her fight with Zeb had shown other ways to use them defensively. "Get him off me," she said.

The Strains grabbed Moldy by the ears and yanked him back. Leilani threw her foot into his groin and broke away. Pocked tackled her, driving his knee into her back. The Strains clashed like breaking glass.

If they kill you, they'll lose the Strains. They won't kill you, Leilani told herself, even as she realized that death was not what she feared from these particular attackers. No, what she feared was far worse.

"Ah, now you really owe me." Moldy stepped over her. Flames crackled at his fingertips.

A bang echoed through the garden. Moldy cried out and clutched his arm. The smell of blood and smoke burned Leilani's nostrils. Moldy's light went out, and Pocked leaped up. Still winded, Leilani scrambled to her feet as a figure stepped out of the darkness, smoking pistol leveled at Moldy. Capped's hands flared to reveal a scowling Brick. Leilani's heart leaped.

Capped pointed at him. "Jump him before he can reload!"

He rushed Brick, but the guard side-stepped and brought the handle of his gun down with a crack on Capped's head. The boy fell with a groan. Brick stuck his pistol back in his belt and drew his saber. Moldy growled and raised his hand. A wave of Strains sang forth, forcing Leilani to the ground. It bounced back from Brick, repelled by his Strain-proof cuffs. Capped struggled to his feet, only to have Brick kick him into the shrubbery. He lay still.

Pocked and Moldy took off running. Brick sheathed his blade. Leilani picked herself up and embraced him. He patted her back, his face pressed into her hair. With the Highmost thugs gone, darkness surrounded them, but his warmth calmed Leilani's pounding heart.

Brick drew a light tube, identical to the one Leilani had used in the tunnels, out of his pocket and shook it to life. He helped her gather up her belongings, including Goodly's cloak, and motioned with his chin and thumb back towards the bridge.

"I'm going to the Cathedral," she explained.

He repeated the movements. She shrugged and nodded. He slipped an arm about her waist, pulling her close to him as they walked. They crossed the bridge back into the Manor District.

Weariness trickled like water through her muscles, pooling in her feet. It became difficult to raise them. Brick took a side path, around Civics Manor. A line of narrow, three story buildings, servants' quarters maybe, stood before her. A group of Common folk sat around a fire-pit in the yard. One, an older man, looked up when they approached. He crowed with laughter and slapped his thigh.

"Look, Brick's brought a lady friend home. Good going, boy. I told you the uniform would work."

Brick waved and drew Leilani to a red painted door on the

first story. He knocked. A woman with gray streaked dark curls and Brick's eyes opened the door. She raised her eyebrows.

"Brick, aren't you supposed to be on duty tonight?" The woman signed as she talked, but Leilani was too weary to catch the movements. The woman pulled them into her one-room home.

A rocking chair sat in front of a pot bellied stove. On top of a wooden table in the center of the room, an oil lamp cast a golden glow over a basket of yarn and a half knitted sweater. There was a basin in a corner with a long-handled pump below a shelf stacked with earthenware dishes. A bouquet of dried flowers hung from the ceiling.

A curtain hid the back end of the apartment, probably concealing her sleeping quarters. There were few possessions, even by Common standards, but the sparseness immediately drew Leilani's eye to a shelf filled with wooden figurines. An elegant swan made of pale wood stood beside a tumbling bear-cub. A pair of horses pranced behind a row of ducklings, and a young girl sat gazing up at a chicken perched upon her head. All looked as if they could spring to life at any moment.

Brick released her so he could work his fingers. Drawn to the statuettes, she listened absently to the spoken half of the conversation, as the woman continued to speak and sign simultaneously.

"Oh, that's *her* . . . Is she all right? . . . they tried to do *what*? Are *you* all right? . . . You shot . . . no, nevermind, I don't want to know . . . she can stay here tonight. Go ask Mrs. Fiest to lend us her spare cot."

The door opened and closed.

She focused on one of the carvings. A wooden girl, captured mid-stride, her arms swinging at her sides. Something stirred in her head. It was like looking in a tiny wooden mirror.

"He brought that home yesterday. Apparently you've been on his mind a good deal of late."

Leilani jumped at the woman's voice in her ear then

blushed.

"My name is Flory Webber. I'm Brick's mother." Flory took the statue down and handed it to Leilani.

Leilani stroked the polished wood. She could see the individual strands of her hair and each tiny finger. "He made me look so pretty. Are all of these his?"

"Yes, he's always been gifted. He almost joined Art Manor. They take a certain amount of Common artisans every year, but for a deaf man to be accepted is unheard of. I was so proud."

Leilani glanced at her. "Why didn't he go?"

Florly lowered her eyes. "His father died unexpectedly. The manor position offered room and board, but nothing extra, and the guard's salary included a home for immediate family. He wanted to make sure I was cared for. I take in laundry or mending from time to time, but it isn't much. At seventeen, he should be starting his own family, not stuck looking after me."

Leilani cleared her throat. "I doubt he thinks of himself as stuck. He seems happy."

Flory smiled. "Oh, he is irrepressible. I couldn't ask for a better son."

The door behind them opened with a whoosh of frigid air. Brick shoved in a long, folding cot. Flory pointed to the floor at her feet. He set it down.

"I'll get some blankets. You both must be exhausted."

Flory spread several threadbare quilts over the cot and offered Leilani some brown bread. As she ate, the girl heard the faint tolling of the Weather Manor clock tower.

"Goodness, midnight already. Brick, you can't walk back so late." Leilani watched Flory walk her fingers up her arm, shaking her head. She tilted her head to the side, closed her eyes, then opened them and pointed to the curtain area. "You'll sleep here."

Brick and his mother disappeared behind the divider.

Leilani slipped off her boots and flexed her toes. Though she had a nightgown, it seemed inappropriate to undress with only a thin wall of cloth between her and Brick.

Able to think for the first time that night, she wondered if Goodly had sent him. The captain must have at least told Brick of what had happened, though perhaps rumor had made its way through other conduits. Kasan struck her as a gossip, the meddling little sneak. Had Brash been behind Kasan's snitching? The fellow hadn't been there, but Kasan didn't breathe without Brash's approval.

Leilani didn't trust Brash. She didn't like his manner with Zeb. Now that Leilani couldn't protect her, who knew what he might try? Zeb needed her.

But Zeb wasn't her friend any more, so that didn't really matter.

Leilani tucked herself in, staring at the low light of the oil lamp.

What will Mother and Father say when I come home? I failed. They probably won't say anything, pretend it never happened . . . oh, but what will they ***think?***

Her spine arched off the taut canvas of the cot. She turned to her side and her hipbone rubbed. She groaned. She put one quilt beneath and one above herself. Marginally better.

The Strains droned, their music twisting in time with the flickering flame. She coaxed faces into the smoke, trying to use the Strains like before. Still, the memory of their screams haunted her, jarring her out of concentration. She shuddered.

Sliding off the cot, she huddled in her blanket. No Zeb. No future. No plan. What now? What next? She combed through her hair with her fingers. Her scalp ached where Zeb had pulled her hair. Stupid Zeb. Stupid Highmost.

The floorboards creaked. Brick strode around the curtain, his leather uniform removed to reveal a gray linen shirt, untucked and loose about his hips and gray leggings. He tilted his head, hand against his cheek, then shook his head 'no.'

She smiled. "Can't sleep?"

He nodded.

"Me either. I learned this." She walked her fingers up her arm. "Go or walk, right?"

He laughed and gave her a thumbs up.

"Was your father deaf?"

He held up a finger, drew a line across his upper lip then rocked his arms as if holding a baby.

"Father?" She carefully made the same motion.

With his finger, he drew a line from his ear to his mouth.

"Deaf?"

He grinned.

She grimaced and rubbed her forehead. "Well, that's two more. If I keep up at this rate, by the time I'm thirty, we'll be able to hold a decent conversation."

His mouth twisted, and he tilted his head. She realized she'd turned her face away, and he hadn't gotten any of what she said. Probably for the best.

She angled herself back towards him. "So he was deaf. But not your mother, obviously? I wonder how . . ." She bit her bottom lip and pulled the quilt closer to her neck.

Brick sat beside her and touched the back of her hand.

"It would be hard," she whispered. His brow furrowed. She pointed to him then touched her chest. "Hard. Difficult."

He shook his head, stroked her cheek, and guided her hand to rest over his heart. Closing her eyes, she concentrated on his pulse. Though she could not hear it with her ears, each beat throbbed through her palm, up her arm. Her breathing synced with his. A contented sigh escaped her lips.

The Strains mixed with the crackling of the fire, a haunting, soothing melody of panpipes and summer breeze, perhaps the loveliest she'd ever heard them.

She opened her eyes and found him gazing back at her. He smiled a warm, slight smile, not his usual boisterous grin, but one that seemed to regret the words he couldn't say. His fingers squeezed her wrist, gentle but strong. His gray eyes gleamed.

I know you. You aren't just a man. You're a man who

would give up a dream for a loved one. Who thinks I can do things even I doubt and who guides me with his hands while I learn. Your eyes light up when they see me. You risked your life to protect me. You've lived your whole life in silence, but I've never seen you afraid. You're brave and wonderful, and I do know you.

You're Brick, and I love you. Oh, how do I say any of that?

She swallowed, her mouth twisting. How could she mime love? What motions could possibly convey what she felt? Perhaps he could read her lips. Her lips . . . Realizing what she wanted to do, she leaned closer to him and touched his mouth with her fingertips. He gazed at her, his pupils widening. She closed her eyes, lifted her face to his, and waited.

Her breath lingered in her lungs, her lips tight together lest it escape. A few seconds passed. Had he not understood? Did he not want to? She let her air go and opened her eyes. He smiled and moved forward, pressing his mouth into hers. His eyes captured her. His arms encircled and drew her closer. Her whole world faded into warmth.

She slid onto his lap, one hand against his chest, one arm around his neck. They parted. She exhaled. While her mouth was still agape, he came for her again. Her fingers grabbed his unruly curls and tightened.

After a long moment he withdrew. His eyes twinkled. She blushed. He brought his right hand to his chest and drew a slow circle with his thumb then touched her face. Somehow she knew immediately what this meant.

"I love you too," she said.

His smile widened. He nodded. They sat, hand and hand. She rested her head on his shoulder, and he eased himself down beside her. Sheltered together in the quilt like two chicks in a nest, they slept.

Chapter Twenty-One

Some time in the early morning, Leilani felt Brick lift her back onto the cot and tuck the quilt about her body. She reached out to pull him back but missed. Her eyes stayed shut, and she sank into dreams.

Leilani woke to the gray light pouring through the room's only window onto her face. She heard the scraping of a wooden spoon against a pot, a sound so familiar that for a moment she imagined she was home. Her arm flopped over the edge of her cot, and it all came flooding back to her.

The screaming Strains, the fight with Zeb, Brick . . .

She glanced around the room. Flory stood by the stove. The curtain had been pushed back, revealing an ancient bronze day bed with a pull out mattress stowed beneath it.

Flory turned. "Good morning. Brick went to find the milk cart. I like milk with my tea." A kettle sang out as if in response.

"So do I." Leilani stood. The floors chilled her toes, so she sat back down and replaced her boots.

Someone rapped at the door.

"Would you get that, Miss Leilani?" Flory poured the kettle's contents through a metal strainer sitting over a chipped china teapot. "Brick probably forgot his key again."

Leilani's face warmed at the mention of his name. She wondered how much Flory knew.

Leilani forced herself to walk to the door, rather than rush it like a child eager to unwrap a present. She opened it, and her hands dropped to her sides.

Zeb stared back, her eyes puffy above purple half circles. She smiled, then frowned, then smiled again.

Leilani folded her arms over her chest. "How did you find me?"

"I asked Captain Goodly. He said he sent Brick after you and gave me this address."

Flory came up behind Leilani. "Oh, hello, may I help you?"

"I need to talk to Leilani, alone. It's rather important."

Leilani sighed, nodded, and retrieved Goodly's cloak. Though oversized, it was thicker and warmer than her own clothes.

The girls strode into the courtyard. In the daylight, the brick houses looked homier. Laundry hung overhead, and potted plants, most past their prime and bound with twine for the winter, cluttered the ledges. Some embers still glowed in the firepit, and the girls settled there. The Strains murmured like running water, soothing and calm.

"They're trying to comfort me, us, I suppose. I don't feel like being comforted, though. Everything's gone so wrong." Zeb kicked a loose coal, avoiding Leilani's eyes. "Anyway, it's my fault. I am sorry I didn't stand up for you last night."

"If you had, both of us would have most likely been kicked out of the manor." As Leilani said it, she grudgingly realized it was true. Mistress Straight had been in no mood to show mercy.

"At least we would've been together. That was the whole point of having you as my aide, and I bumbled it." Zeb sniffed, her nose shiny red in the winter air. "I thought it would bring us closer, make us inseparable, but then the Strains and Brick–"

"Don't start on Brick again!" Leilani scowled.

"No, no, that isn't . . ." Zeb gave a whistling exhale. "He really likes you, doesn't he?"

Leilani nodded. "More than likes."

Zebedy grimaced. "I want to be happy for you, Leilani, but I'm miserable. You know, my parents are wonderful, but all they ever talk about is the almanac, what they'll write for weather predictions, planting guidelines. Before you, the only person I had to talk to wasn't even a person at all."

"The Strains?"

"Yes, and now I might lose them and you at the same time. When I saw how Brick looked at you, my stomach started twisting. No one is ever going to look at me that way. Ever. When you marry Brick, I'll just be alone."

Leilani grasped Zeb's shoulder. "First, no one is getting married anytime soon. Second, no, you won't be alone. You are gorgeous and brilliant."

"And odd." Zeb snorted.

"Well, yes." Leilani smiled. "But I've never minded that, and I can think of at least one Civics fellow who doesn't either."

The red in Zeb's nose flooded her face. "Now you're just being mean. Vickers . . . anyway, that isn't important. What matters is that you can't hate me. I'd go mad."

Leilani pulled her friend into a hug. "I will never hate you. I may want to slap you sometimes, but in a loving way."

Zeb laughed and squeezed back. "I want to try and get you your position back. Brash will understand you were acting to save the Strains. Once you tell him what you saw, he'll be able to fix things. Everything will go back to normal."

"They won't let me just come back. Mistress Straight isn't letting me anywhere near her precious manor."

Zeb clutched her hands together. "I'll resign then, but we need to at least try."

Leilani swallowed. "I will talk to Brash with you, but we need to be careful. Kasan was the one who reported me to Straight. Brash could be involved."

Zeb looked past Leilani. "Would it make you feel better if we brought *him*?"

Leilani followed Zeb's gaze. Brick strode across the courtyard, a milk bottle in his hand. She watched him enter his mother's house.

"It would," she agreed.

The girls walked towards the house, but Zeb paused when she touched the doorknob. "I sent a message to Vickers this morning. After what happened in the tunnels last night, I figured we needed to get back, even if Straight wouldn't listen."

Leilani bit her bottom lip. "Will he be able to overrule Straight?"

"Straight has a lot of influence in Research, but Vickers should be able to get us past her, because of his project about the tunnels but also because once Straight hears his last name, she'll melt into a kowtowing puddle." Zeb snorted. "No one in the manors would say no to a Buffet."

"Except you." Leilani chuckled. "Though maybe you should reconsider that."

Zeb blushed again and opened the door.

Flory had set the table for four, each place with a bowl of steaming porridge and a tea cup.

"I didn't know if your friend would be staying or not," she said.

"I've already eaten, but I would be grateful for a cup of tea, thank you." Zeb smiled.

Brick circled the table, pulling out chairs for each lady in turn.

"Brick was just telling me that his captain has given him the day off to see to Miss Leilani." Flory stirred sugar into her tea. Brick shoveled several spoonfuls onto his porridge. She frowned at him, but her eyes twinkled.

"I'm Zebedy. I didn't catch your name, Miss. . .?" Zebedy glanced at Flory over her teacup and took a sip.

"Just Flory, dear."

Zeb leaned closer to Leilani. "Maybe she can help us explain everything to Brick."

Brick set down his spoon.

"If you need to tell Brick something, I will help. He reads mouths well, but signs better," Flory said.

"What does he know about the Strains?" Zeb asked. "Our story involves them a good deal."

"He has seen others wield them," Flory explained, watching Brick's hands. Brick touched his ear, shook his head, then tapped his forehead and nodded yes. Flory laughed. "He says just because he cannot hear does not mean he cannot think."

Leilani tried not to smirk at Zeb's blush.

"Something is destroying the Strains," Leilani began.

Brick alternated between watching Zeb's mouth and his mother's fingers, nodding occasionally. Zeb explained about the dead spots and the amplifiers then allowed Leilani to relate what she'd seen in the tunnels. Flory's face turned white.

"I can't imagine someone doing that to the Strains," she whispered. Brick touched her hand. "Have you tried getting help?"

"We tried telling Cogg, then Straight. No one wants to listen. Brash said he would help," Zeb said.

"And you want Brick to go with you to see this Brash?" Flory dropped her eyes. "It sounds dangerous. I have already lost so much."

Brick took his mother aside after breakfast. This time Flory did not speak as they conversed. Leilani and Zeb cleared away the dishes. Zeb had no idea how to wash a bowl, and instructing her kept Leilani's eyes off their farewell.

"I think I could use the Strains for this," Zeb said as she whisked a towel over a plate.

Leilani rolled her eyes. "You don't need to use the Strains for every little thing."

"But I *could*." Zeb took the next clean spoon from Leilani. "Anyway, do we even need to dry them? The air does that."

"Just do it." Leilani pushed a teacup at Zeb who grimaced but obeyed.

Brick approached and pointed to the door.

"Time to go," Zeb said. "Hopefully Brash can make some sense of this."

"I just want to get back into the tunnels and dismantle those devices." Leilani gathered up her things, and the three of them started out.

Vendors with carts and folk hurrying to and from the various manors filled the streets. The Strains swelled when they passed a large group of people, happy and carefree as if the night before hadn't happened. With Zeb and Brick flanking her and the Strains loud and clear, Leilani felt brave again.

The guards at Research Manor nodded to Brick and thankfully didn't give Leilani a second glance. She breathed a sigh of relief. She had worried Mistress Straight might have ordered them to keep her out.

"Brash will be in his workshop. Classes start in less than an hour." Zeb pointed to the building.

The door stood ajar in spite of the cold winter morning. Zeb's pace quickened, but Brick grabbed her arm. His eyebrows drew together. He pointed to the door, walked his fingers up his arm, then tapped his chest and held up one finger. He touched the hilt of his saber and started forward.

Zeb glanced at Leilani. "What is he afraid of?"

Leilani shrugged. "He's a guard. Probably just being cautious." But the hairs on the back of her neck stood on end. The Strains wailed, still melodious, but in a loud, minor key.

Brick kicked the door and stepped inside. A moment later he emerged, face grave, and beckoned them in.

The girls passed him into the workshop then froze. On the floor, her face pale and her eyes staring at the ceiling, lay Straight. A trail of blood trickled from her ear and crusted in her hair.

Cold chills swept through Leilani. Zeb made a gagging sound and doubled over.

Leilani jumped when Brick placed his hand on her shoulder.

"What happened?" Her voice shook, and her hands trembled. She scanned the room. All the vials and jars on the workbenches and several panes in the windows had been shattered. She stepped closer, into a dead spot. "The Strains did this."

Zeb straightened up. "That's insane. The Strains can't kill people. They *wouldn't.*"

Leilani grasped her friend's arm and pulled her into the emptiness. Zeb's breath escaped in a silent shriek, and she pushed Leilani away.

Zeb hugged herself, shrinking away from Leilani. "What are you doing?"

"Trying to get it through your thick skull that this is real. Someone has weaponized the Strains, and considering this, it is a safe bet it is Brash."

Wide-eyed, Zeb shook her head. "It couldn't be him. He passed the Strains test . . ."

"So did I when Straight caught me, and we both know how." Leilani crossed her arms over her chest.

"But I trust him!"

"Well, where is he?" Leilani stuck her hands on her hips.

Zeb scanned the room, her mouth clamped shut.

Leilani turned to Brick and fished out her notepad again. She wrote and spoke, as much for Zeb's benefit as his. "We have to get into the tunnels. Whatever he's doing, that's where he'll be."

Brick nodded. He tugged up his sleeves and undid the clasps on his wristlets. He held one out to Leilani and the other to Zeb. Leilani shook her head even as Zeb took hers.

Leilani pushed the cuff away. "No, then what will protect you?"

Brick smiled a cocky smile and tapped his saber hilt. He fastened the silver cuff around Leilani's wrist. It fit loosely. Wherever the metal touched, her skin tingled. The Strains still sang to her, but they sounded muffled, as if she had water in her ears.

Zeb put hers on and shuddered. "Oh, I don't like that."

Leilani resisted the urge to pop her ears. "He's right, though. If the Strains are weaponized, we need all the help we can get."

Brick pointed to Straight's body, touched his lips, then saluted.

Leilani nodded. "Yes, we should tell Captain Goodly. We can't just leave her like this."

"Leave who like this . . . by the Strains! What happened?" Goodly rushed through the door and knelt by Straight's body. He touched the side of her neck. He glanced up at the three young folk. "What do you know about this?" he signed as he spoke. Brick made several rapid hand motions.

"We were looking for Brash and found her like this," Leilani said. "Brash must've done it."

Goodly's brow furrowed. "That is a serious accusation, Miss Leilani. Do you have any proof?"

Leilani bit her bottom lip. "No, but *she's* here."

"As are you. I have only your word that this is how you found her."

"Strains test us, then!" Zeb exclaimed. "I don't know if it was Brash, but it certainly wasn't us."

Goodly exhaled loudly and stood. "That would clear you, but unfortunately, not Brick. Come with me, all of you. We will sort this out." He stepped towards them.

Leilani backed away. "We can't. We have to get to the tunnels. Brash will be there."

"Brash isn't even in the Manor. He canceled his classes today. That's why the open door caught my eye. Now, please, let's go talk this out."

"It could be too late by then." Leilani grabbed Brick's arm. The young guard glanced from his superior to her. "Run," she mouthed. He raised his eyebrows.

Goodly's hand grazed his saber hilt.

Zeb's frame stiffened. "You have to listen."

"No, you do." Goodly's frown deepened. He signed as he spoke. "Brick, come with me, or I will put you and your friends all under arrest. Hand me your saber and pistol."

Brick's jaw dropped.

Goodly raised his hands then continued to sign. "I don't like it either, and I believe you are innocent. However, there are protocols for such situations. We need to follow them. Come with me, and we'll have this cleared up in a few hours."

Brick began signing furiously.

"Whatever is going on can wait," Goodly said. "Your weapons. Now."

Zeb's eyes met Leilani's. Zeb's nose wrinkled, and her lips moved in an inaudible whisper.

The Strains trilled shrilly. With a clatter, Brash's wheeled table skidded across the floor. It bounced off the shield created by Goodly's wristlets, but he turned towards it, breaking his stare from Brick.

"Run!" Zeb shrieked.

Leilani pushed Brick. He stumbled out the door. Zeb shoved it shut and used the Strains to lock it.

Leilani grabbed Brick's right hand and Zeb his left, and somehow they got him to run. By the time they reached the tunnel gate, Leilani's side ached. She placed her hands on her knees and gulped air. Somewhat steadier, she turned her attention to the lock.

Zeb sank to the floor. "What was I thinking? Oh Strains, what was I thinking?"

Brick stood a few feet away, casting his gaze up then down the hall. He didn't seem winded from the run, but his gray eyes looked wounded.

Oh what did I get him into?

Leilani's pin hit the last tumbler, and she opened the gate. "Let's go."

Zeb lit her fingers. Brick took Leilani's hand, and they walked through the darkness to the first fork. Leilani stopped. The floor down both paths had been swept clean, leaving no tracks.

"Which way?" Zeb asked.

Leilani hesitated. She remembered the first fork. Right, she thought. No, *knew*. She *knew* it was right. However, each choice after that grew progressively fuzzier.

Zeb closed her eyes. "What do you think? You were here with her. Do you remember?" She opened her eyes and smiled. "This way."

With Zeb in the lead, they navigated the twists and turns, finally arriving at the ladder to the pillar room.

"And without Vickers's maps and compasses." Zeb beamed.

Leilani glanced down the tube. No light shone below. "Perhaps Brash isn't here after all."

"I still want to see these devices." Zeb held up her glowing fingers. "Makes sense for me to go first."

As first Zeb, then Brick, lowered themselves into the hole, Leilani concentrated on the Strains. They sounded calm, like her mother's humming.

"We're going to save you," she whispered. She descended into the darkness.

Zeb investigated the machines in the middle of the room, her light illuminating a few yards about her. Brick stood in the darkness at the bottom of the ladder. He grasped Leilani about the waist to help her down the last little bit.

"Oh, this is diabolical," Zeb said as Leilani and Brick reached her. "Somehow they condense and store the Strains, like a gas. These dials display the pressure. Oh my. That's way too high." Zeb stepped back. "I think they are off. If they were going, this room, and everything above it, would be a dead spot."

"I saw the man filling a smaller canister from these," Leilani said. "When he threw it at me, it exploded."

"This reminds me of Verge's focus boxes. Remember how he accidentally blinded an aide then demolished his workshop? His boxes were on a much smaller scale than this. If these went off, it would take a chunk out of the manor above."

Brick tapped Zeb on the shoulder and raised his palms in

the air.

She bit her bottom lip. “Can I have your notepad, Leilani?”

Leilani raised her eyebrows but handed over her writing utensils.

Zeb scratched out a note and passed it to Brick.

His eyes grew wide. He put his hands together then threw them apart.

Leilani’s heart felt cold. “Do you think that’s their purpose? To blow up the manor?”

“Oh no, from what you said, they are collecting Strains to use elsewhere. It is still dangerous, but there are any number of harmless reasons to do that. Concentrated Strains have a myriad of uses.” Zeb passed Brick a second note, and Leilani had to smile.

At least she's trying.

After reading it, Brick shook his head, held up two fingers, then slashed across his neck.

“He’s right.” Leilani nodded. “If it were harmless, they wouldn’t have killed two people to cover it up.”

Zeb shuddered so dramatically her shoulder raised to her ears. She then shook her head and circled the tank, reaching out every so often to touch a knob or a dial. “I can figure these out. Perhaps we can dismantle them, break them.” She knocked on one with her fist, causing a dull clang. “Sturdy, though. We might need tools.”

Leilani swept the edge of the room with her gaze. She saw only shadows. On the wall opposite, a thin yellow line formed a rectangle. Light slipping around a door? She touched Brick’s arm and pointed. He squinted and frowned.

Moving on the balls of his feet, Brick crept towards the door. He kicked it open and dove inside. Someone cried out. There was a crash, then a series of bumps. Leilani and Zeb rushed to the doorway. The space appeared to be a storage room. Shelves filled with crates lined the walls. In the back a lantern sat on a table surrounded by stacks of paper. Brick sat on Brash. The man kicked like a three-year-old having a tantrum.

"Let me go!" Brash snarled, rocking back and forth.

Brick stood and forced Brash to stand. Blood dripped from the fellow's nose.

Zeb took a handkerchief out of her pocket, held it forth, then drew back. Her bottom lip trembled. Brash's burning eyes softened.

"I trusted you," she said.

The Strains swirled about them like buzzing bees, tense and angry.

Brash cleared his throat. "This isn't how it looks."

"You said you would investigate the dead spots when you were causing them in the first place." Leilani crossed her arms over her chest. "That's how it looks."

"Well, that is . . . the dead spots are a momentary inconvenience. What we will gain through this work is immeasurable."

Zeb strode past him to a table. She picked up one piece of paper, scanned it, and selected another. Her brow furrowed.

Leilani came to stand beside her. "What is it?"

"Not what I expected. These look like medical devices." Zeb turned back to Brash. "These schematics show how to use the amplifiers to restore the Strains to the Wordless. Why would you be investigating that?"

Brash dropped his eyes. "I just wanted to hear them again."

The paper fell from Zeb's hand and fluttered to the floor. "But I saw you use the Strains."

"There is a tension wire in my watch chain. Tightening it makes it rigid and--"

"And it looks like it is floating," Zeb whispered. "Oh, I should've seen that."

"It has fooled dozens of folk before you, Miss Brightly. Cogg was the only one to see through it. He let me keep my fellowship, but I have paid through the nose for his silence."

"How long have you been Wordless?" Leilani asked. She disliked the sympathy creeping into her heart. Perhaps Brash had lied, but the loss of the Strains could drive a man mad.

"Almost five years. I had a . . . It was an accident, I swear, a fight between friends that got out of hand. I told the guards he slipped and fell. They never questioned, never guessed that I shoved him. I tried to make amends–"

"Who was he?" Leilani interrupted.

"My first aide, Vern Morgan."

"Kasan's brother?"

"Aye, that's why I hired the lad. Vern's parents died, and Kasan needed someone to provide for him."

"Someone like his brother's murderer?" Leilani's lips curled into a sneer.

"Oh, he never knew. He's even helping me with this, doesn't realize it's for me. Things were going so well. Cogg even agreed to my experiments, saw the potential for greatness in them. Then the dead spots popped up, and he wanted to stop everything. When I was so close!"

"So you killed him?" Leilani raised her eyebrows.

"Our argument grew heated. It was a moment of passion and weakness."

"You seem to have a lot of those."

Brash winced and fell silent.

"What you are doing harms the Strains." Zeb's face grew red. "It's unnatural and cruel. You've made them into *weapons*!"

"You nearly killed me!" Leilani added.

"No, I intentionally missed you." He motioned towards the table with his head. On it sat the cylinder he'd been carrying the night before. "It's a portable collector, but when it gets full I use it to fill up the . . . well, I call them grenades because they explode when you throw them, but they are extremely short ranged. I knew unless you were standing right on top of it, you wouldn't be seriously injured. Making weapons was not my intent, simply a byproduct of the bottling process." Brash shifted from one foot to the other.

Zeb's eyebrows hit her hairline. "Bottling process? They're Strains, not blackberry wine. I should bottle you, you lying, worthless, murderous . . ." She burst into tears. "I trusted you."

"I am so sorry, Miss Brightly. I am such a wretch." He hung his head.

"At least you're self-aware," Leilani muttered.

Brick shrugged, raised two fingers, and pointed to Brash.

Leilani glared at Brash. "He's right, you killed two . . . no, three! Three people! I hope you hang!"

Brash tilted his head to the side, his mouth slightly open. "Three? Two is the correct number. That's not the sort of thing a man miscounts."

"No," Zeb sniffed back tears. "Kasan's brother, Cogg, and Straight: three."

Brash drew a staggering breath. "Straight? Calia Straight? No. What happened to her? We . . . she . . . I would never hurt Calia! She isn't part of this. Why did you say Straight?"

Leilani and Zeb exchanged a glance.

"She was dead in your workshop this morning," Leilani said.

Brash stumbled back against the wall. "No, I never . . . I would never hurt Calia."

"No," said an icy voice behind them. "But I would."

Chapter Twenty-Two

Leilani turned. In the doorway, cloaked in shadow, stood a slight figure. She squinted.

"Kasan?" Brash stammered.

The boy raised a light vial, flooding a face filled with malice. He sneered.

"You killed Calia?" Brash breathed.

"You took something I loved. It was only fair that I returned the favor." Kasan drew a small, metal canister from under his cloak and tossed it lazily up and down.

Brash fell to his knees. "How could you know? You didn't know."

"Obviously, he did," Leilani snapped.

Brick's hand encircled her arm. She eyed the object in Kasan's fingers. Her breath caught in her throat. It was the same as the projectile lobbed at her the day before.

"Kasan, we've caught him," Zeb said. "He'll be punished. You don't have to . . . Everything will be all right. This is over."

Kasan's fist clenched around the Strains grenade. "No, this is just beginning. You Highmost think you can control everything. You act as if you are above us all. No one cared when my brother died, because he was Common. You took my brother's life and nothing happened. Cogg covered it up, for money! As if money could pay for . . ." The aide's shoulders shook. "I have bit my tongue and listened to your hypocrisy for the last time. The manors will fall, all of them, and you, Brash, you gave me the tools to achieve it."

Brash raised his head. "My collectors? What did you do to them?"

"Enough."

"You have more collectors?" Zeb shrieked.

"A grouping under every manor." Kasan grinned. "Brash has always been greedy."

Brick reached towards his holstered pistol.

"I see that," Kasan snarled. He waved his grenade, one finger extended. Brick froze.

"Let them go," Brash said. "What I did to your brother was wrong. I can never make that right, and I am sorry, but these girls had nothing to do with it."

A ripple of rage crossed Kasan's face. "This isn't about Vern any more. No, his death may have started it, but it was a symptom, not the disease itself. The disease is you *Highmost*." He spat out the word. "You isolate yourselves in your manors with no concern for how your playing about affects those beneath you. And why are we beneath you? Not because you work harder, or even smarter, as your constant state of bewilderment has exhibited, but because of the Strains."

The Strains shrieked like a cold wind. Leilani covered her ears against the blast. Zeb let out a sob.

"The Strains divide us. The Strains created the Highmost, created this blight on our entire city. I will take the manors down and the Strains with them. I have the schematics for your collectors now. Once the manors have fallen, I will set them up all over Gelia until the Strains are sucked away entirely."

Leilani's jaw dropped, and Zeb whimpered.

Zeb took a step towards Kasan, but Brash put out a hand to hold her back.

"You can't do this. The Strains are alive. You can't do this to them. They are begging you not to do this. Can't you hear them?" Zeb pleaded.

Kasan shrugged. "Not any longer, and I'm loving the silence." He took a step back, just outside the door. "Sorry girls, nothing personal. Can't have you getting in the way." With a fluid movement, he tossed the grenade and slammed the door shut.

"No!" Brash shouted. He dove towards the projectile.

Brick's body slammed into the girls, knocking them both under the table. The Strains exploded. Leilani felt it bounce off her, deflected by her wristlet. The shrieking of the Strains blended with Zeb's screams. Then silence, terrible, total silence.

Leilani struggled to her feet. Zeb's whimper fought through the ringing in Leilani's ears. Brick's arm moved, though he didn't rise. Her friends accounted for, she knelt by Brash. Blood trickled from the fellow's ears and mouth. His eyes stared blankly up at her, and the shattered remnants of the grenade lay about him.

Zeb sat up, her hands over her ears. Tears ran down her face. Brick rolled over, rubbing his eyes.

Zeb rushed to the door and shook it. "It won't open. What is he doing out there?" She banged on the door. "It's locked from the outside. That blast . . . I can't use the Strains." She slid to the floor, hand resting on her silver cuff. "At least these protected us." She exhaled. "Thanks, Brick."

Brick stared forward. Leilani tapped her chest, remembering the sign. Brick touched his face and reached forward. His hand shook. Leilani's heart chilled.

"What's the matter?" Zeb asked. "He looks stricken."

Leilani knelt at Brick's side. His eyes focused forward, not following her. She touched his shoulder. He jumped and flailed out. Blindly. His hand found hers then felt up her arm to her face.

"Brick," she whispered.

"Let me see him." Zeb came to them. She passed her hand in front of his eyes. He didn't react. "Oh no." Zeb stood, wringing her hands. "He . . . he can't see."

Chapter Twenty-Three

Brick huddled in the corner, his head against Leilani's shoulder. She stroked his hair and kissed his forehead. He no longer shook, but his smile had died. She could not coax it forth.

"You should've kept your bracelets, at least one. It would've protected you. You wouldn't . . ." Her voice cracked.

Zeb twisted her cuff about her wrist, staring at Leilani and the blinded guard. "It doesn't matter. We're running out of time."

Leilani looked up. "What?"

"Kasan." Zeb stood, unfastened her cloak, and laid it over Brash's corpse. "He turned on the collectors. That's why the Strains haven't come back, what he meant when he said the manors would fall." She pressed her body into the door and banged her forehead on the wood. "When the pressure in those canisters builds up, they'll blast a hole through the manor above. The whole building will come down on our heads. We're going to die here, and soon, a few hours at most."

Leilani tightened her grasp on Brick. His warmth gave her strength. Right now he needed her. She couldn't let herself be afraid.

"It must be nice to have him right now." Zeb didn't turn around. "I would've liked that. I'm not scared, you know. Just lonely. My parents will never know what happened to me. Other than you and them . . . I would've liked a chance to love someone. Really, really love. . . like he loves you." She sat crosslegged, her chin in her hands. "I'm so sorry for everything I said about him. He deserves you, and that's the best thing I could imagine saying about anyone. Anyway, I only wish . . . I could say the same about me."

Leilani swallowed and kissed Brick's forehead.

He raised his head. Tears glistened on his cheeks.

"Just pretend I'm not here," Zeb said. "He needs you."

Brick pulled his arms away from Leilani and touched her chin. He waved his hand in a circle about his face, over a broken smile.

"Beautiful," Leilani whispered.

Her heart shattered.

She kissed his lips and rubbed her nose into his cheek.

Zeb stood. "If I had the Strains, I could do something to help him." She slammed her palm against the door frame. "Of course, if I had the Strains I'd rip this from its hinges and get us out of here. Oh, I am so useless without the Strains."

"Zeb, shut up," Leilani said.

Zeb froze.

Leilani laughed half-heartedly. "You are my best friend, and there are a myriad of reasons for that, not one of which involves the Strains. You're smart and vibrant, and in spite of your clueless nature, your heart is in the right place. Even when you're wrong, like you were about Brick or Brash . . . or Vickers."

"I don't want to think about Vickers right now. The funny thing is, though, if I had heard back from him in time, it might've been him and me down here instead of you and me." Zeb snorted. "Now that would've been interesting." She fell silent.

Leilani entwined her fingers with Brick's. "How long . . . what is Kasan's plan? To knock down Research?"

"More than just Research. Brash set up multiple collection sites, disguising them as part of his sensor project, most likely. If he has one under every manor, Kasan could bring them all down one at a time."

Leilani shook her head. "Hundreds will die."

"Thousands, more accurately. He's obviously gone quite mad."

Living with the Highmost can do that to a person, Leilani thought, though she didn't say it. Yes, the Highmost could be frustrating and intolerant, but they didn't deserve to die for it.

Leilani pried herself from Brick's embrace.

He adjusted his arms to hug himself and bent forward.

"This is ridiculous," she said "I'm not going to just sit here. There must be something we can do."

She pulled a crate from the shelves. Canisters, copper tubes, glass jars . . . She pushed it aside and went for another.

Zeb joined her. "What are we looking for?"

"A crowbar, a hammer, anything to open that door." Leilani threw a box of parchment across the floor. It bumped into the table Brick leaned against, and he jumped. Leilani almost went to him, but the screech of rusty nails made her glance back at Zeb.

Zeb pried the lid off another container. "A gross of quill pens. These supplies are ancient. The manors have only stocked fountain pens for the last two decades."

Leilani rolled her eyes. "Thanks for the history lesson." She climbed up onto the second shelf to reach the top. The wooden shelf swayed beneath her.

"Whoa!" Zeb pushed it back against the wall.

Leilani glanced down the line of crates. All appeared to be nailed shut. On the top of the last, however, coated with dust and cobwebs, sat a rusty hammer. She cried out for joy and batted at it with her fingertips. It clattered to the floor, and she jumped down after it.

Zeb's eyes brightened. "Yes! Yes!"

Leilani grasped the wooden handle of the pitted, metal tool. She wedged the claw in between the door and the frame and pulled. A chunk of wood flew out of the frame, and she fell backwards onto her tailbone. Grunting, she stood and attacked the door again. Once more she chipped the frame, but the door stayed shut.

"Maybe turn the hammer around," Zeb said.

"How would that make a difference. Here you try." Leilani handed her the tool. "You weigh more than me. You'll get better leverage."

Zeb wrinkled her nose. "I don't weigh *that* much more than you." She wedged the claw end of the hammer in place and pushed with her whole body.

Snap!

She toppled, the handle of the hammer still in her hand and the head stuck the door. She whimpered, shrieked, and raised the metal tipped handle like a blade, hacking into the door. Splinters flew.

"Zeb! Zeb!" Leilani gasped, afraid to step closer.

Her friend continued the assault on the wood, sobbing uncontrollably.

A piece of wood arched across the room and hit Brick. He inhaled sharply, and Leilani hurried to comfort him. He clutched her hand and scrambled to his feet, feeling forward.

"No, sit." She tried to push him back down, worried he'd stumble into Zeb's rampage. He shook his head and pointed towards the door. She couldn't explain that they were trapped . . . and about to die . . . or anything. She collapsed into him with a long suppressed sob. His fingers trailed across her damp cheek, and he shook his head. His arms surrounded her. She clutched his shirt and closed her eyes, wishing once more he had kept the wristlets, and she had been the one who had been blinded.

"Zebedy?" a muffled voice called.

The frantic sounds of Zeb's assault on the door stopped. Leilani's eyes widened, and she turned. Brick's arms stayed around her waist like a belt.

"We're in here!" Zeb called. "It's locked. We can't get out."

Leilani heard the grating of a rusty deadbolt, and the door swung open.

Vickers stepped into the room, a lantern in one hand. He set it down and put his hands on Zeb's shaking shoulders. "Are you all right?"

"How?" She gaped at him.

He glanced at the body on the floor, grimaced, then

cleared his throat. "Your letter. When I got it, I came right away to see you, and Goodly was spouting some nonsense that you killed someone and locked him in a room and disappeared into thin air." He wiped the back of his hand across his forehead. "They were putting together a search team, when all hell broke loose. Those dead spots you mentioned are everywhere. They've consumed the entirety of Research Manor. They started evacuating, and that gave me the chance to come look for you. I knew you were somewhere in the tunnels. I've been looking for almost an hour now."

Zeb gasped and pulled away from him. "The collectors!"

She rushed out into the middle of the room. Vickers took up his lamp and followed. Leilani urged Brick forward, her arm hooked into his.

"Zeb," she called out. "If it is going to explode we need to get out of here, now."

"Explode?" Vickers staggered back a step. "What are these things?"

"I can fix them," Zeb growled. "The pressure needs to be evened out. It's just an issue of . . ." She opened a valve, and Strains escaped with a whistle like a teapot.

Vickers covered his ears.

"Everyone, look for valves. Open the valves!" Zeb ordered.

Vickers sprang to life, moving with a speed that belied his usual, laid back demeanor.

Leilani started towards them, but Brick's fingers clenched into her wrist. The sound of the escaping Strains became unbearable, like a whirlwind of ghosts. Leilani's hair whipped into her face, and Brick pulled her tightly against himself. Vickers and Zeb collided at the last collector, tripping over each other to get to the handles.

Zeb clutched the valve, twisted it, and collapsed onto the floor. Vickers leaned against the collector with one hand. His chest rose and fell in a visible sigh. The swirling Strains died to a whisper.

"These caused the dead spots, didn't they?" he asked.

Zeb nodded, hugging herself. Tears poured down her cheeks.

He took her hand and pulled her up. "Hey, are you all right?"

She shook her head. "Everything has gone so terribly, terribly wrong." She sniffed, hiccuped, and huffed out a long breath.

"Well, it's all over now, whatever *it* was." Vickers dusted his hands on his pants. "I know you didn't kill anyone, but you should come up and be Strains tested, as soon as these dead spots fade, that is, just to prove it to Goodly."

"But it isn't over! He's going to . . . Oh, I'll explain on the way. Leilani, can Brick travel?"

"Yes, if I help him."

"Good. Let's get him some place safe and try to get word to the other manors before it is too late."

Chapter Twenty-Four

Except for an occasional raised eyebrow, Vickers remained expressionless as Zeb related recent events. Leilani carefully guided Brick through the tunnels, keeping close to Vickers's lantern. Dead spots still consumed the majority of the space they passed through.

"I never thought Brash could be a killer, let alone Kasan," Zeb concluded.

"All it takes for a man to be a killer is another man in the room," Vickers said dryly.

They reached the gate, and Brick and Leilani pulled ahead when Vickers tried to lead them towards the guard house, and Zeb stopped to argue.

Heavy silence filled the grand halls of Research, giving the manor a sepulchral mood. Leilani helped Brick to a rounded bench at the crossroads of two corridors. He sat, his fingers gripping the edge of the seat.

Vickers and Zeb came up behind them, bickering.

"We need to tell the guards," Vickers said.

"By the time we convince Goodly that we didn't kill Straight, it could be too late. We need to dismantle the collectors ourselves, before the manors start to crumble around us."

Vickers pushed past her and knelt in front of Brick. He waved his hand before the guard's eyes and bit his lip. "No pupil reaction. There hasn't been a case of Strains-induced blindness in decades. My father might be able to help him."

"If Healing Manor is destroyed, your father won't be helping anyone." Leilani suppressed her hope, forcing herself to focus on the problems at hand.

Vickers stood. "I understand if you want to stay with him.

He needs you now. Zebedy, you should stay here as well. I know my way around the tunnels. I will take care of it."

Zeb scowled. "Just like a man. Come in to save the day and push us to the side. We can take care of this, Vicky. Or can you not hear me over the whistling through my ears?"

Vickers's face darkened. "Can you pull your head out of the sand?" He grasped her by the shoulders.

Instead of pulling away, she stuck her chin at him, her eyes smoldering.

"I'm trying to help you," he said through clenched teeth.

"By taking over? No, thank you."

Leilani stood, ready to push her way in between them.

"It's dangerous." His eyebrows melted together.

"No more so for me than you. I've handled myself just fine so far–"

He snorted. "By getting yourself locked in a closet?"

"We would have gotten out," Zeb said, though Leilani knew she was lying.

Zeb's eyes burned into him. "Give me one good reason why you should go instead of us."

"I don't want to see you hurt!" Vickers's breath came out ragged and something in Zeb's eyes softened. He pulled her up and forward and pressed his lips to hers.

Leilani stepped back, nearly tripping over the bench. *He finally . . . oh what will Zeb do?*

Zeb didn't fight it. Vickers lifted her off the ground, and her fingers clutched at his shirt. She went limp. After a long moment they separated, but their gazes stayed fixed.

He flushed, lowered his eyes, and released her. "I'm sorry. I shouldn't have." He rubbed the back of his neck.

She trailed her fingers across his jawline. "No, you . . . I'm glad you did. I just thought . . . Never mind. Again?" She held her face up to him.

Well, apparently she likes it. Good for them. Leilani cleared her throat. "I hate to break this up, but the manors?"

"Oh! The manors!" Zeb's eyes snapped open. She pulled away from Vickers, but he grabbed her by the wrist.

"If something happens to you, I'll never forgive myself," he said.

She ruffled his hair. "If the manors fall, I'll never forgive myself. You know I can do this."

He brushed his palm against her cheek. "Yes, I do. Please, be careful, though."

Leilani kissed Brick's forehead. "There are five remaining manors and three of us. If we want to stop Kasan, we'll need to split up."

Vickers turned to face her. "The layout of the tunnels is identical beneath each manor. The room the collectors were in is called the market room. When the tunnels were well trafficked, vendors would camp there. There is one beneath every manor. It is likely those are the rooms where he placed the collectors. I know my way best around Civics and Healing. Zeb, I'm assuming you know Weather."

Zeb nodded.

"I'll take Art," Leilani said. She laid her hand on Brick's knee.

Zeb touched Vickers's arm. "You could get to Healing before you could reach Civics, and backtracking from Healing to Civics will take time. I can do Weather and Civics. If the collectors aren't on yet, do what you can to damage them. Leilani, you can take Industry once you're done with Art."

Vickers eyed Brick. "Give me his pistol, ammunition pouch, and saber."

Brick grunted as if Leilani had punched him in the stomach when she disarmed him but did not resist. Her insides quivered at seeing him so helpless. She couldn't leave him alone . . . but if she didn't press on, how many more would be hurt?

"I don't suppose either of you know how to shoot?" Vickers asked, taking the pistol and pouch from Leilani. Both girls shook their heads. He tucked the gun into his belt. "One of the advantages of being with Civics, I've played with these toys before. Which of you wants the blade?"

"I'll take it," Leilani said when Zeb hesitated. She slipped the saber into her messenger bag. It protruded from the top, but if she held it close to her side, no one would notice.

"Hopefully, though, killing won't be necessary," Vickers said. "Kasan should be Wordless. You can use the Strains to disable him. It won't be lethal–they won't allow for it–but they will let you restrain him, and he shouldn't be able to fight back. Surprise is your friend. Be swift. Be quiet. Take him down before he sees you. I want both of you alive at the end of the day, all right?"

His bossiness irked Leilani, but surprisingly, Zeb beamed at him. Leilani chose to keep her mouth shut.

Vickers motioned to Brick. "Are you sure you don't want to stay, Leilani?"

"Want to, yes." Leilani swallowed.

Vickers glanced down the hall then back at her. "I'll take Industry off your hands. Just see to Art and come back to him."

Her heart eased, and she forgave Vickers for his assertiveness.

Zeb and Vickers departed together. Leilani lingered. She guided Brick's hand over her heart then brought it to her mouth. "I will be back," she whispered though she knew he couldn't hear.

He grasped at the air when she pulled away, then forced his mouth into a firm line and sat, staring into nothing.

Leilani did not look back. She knew if she did, it would steal her strength and break her heart.

Chapter Twenty-Five

Leilani caught up with Zeb and Vickers just as the pair parted ways outside Research. Vickers bent down and touched his lips to Zeb's forehead before turning towards Healing.

Zeb watched him for a moment then joined Leilani. The Strains swelled to meet them in a chorus of bells, and the dull ache behind Leilani's breastbone eased somewhat.

Zeb's posture relaxed. "Finally, they're back. Let's hurry. I can't let that happen to them again."

The girls walked at a brisk pace. Zeb started to run, but Leilani grabbed her arm. "For all we know Goodly has put out warrants for our arrest. We can't draw attention to ourselves."

Zeb nodded, her lips pursed. "I'm not meant for the life of a fugitive. I always manage to draw attention to myself. At least we can stick together until Art. Why did you choose it, anyway? 'Cause it's closer?"

"It was the first to come to mind. Maybe because Brick loves art." Leilani cleared her throat. "He wants to be a sculptor."

"Oh, that makes it so much worse." Zeb's mouth tightened. "We'll fix this, Leilani. I swear, we will fix this."

The girls maintained a quick pace. They kept their heads down, but no one seemed to be looking at them.

"First Research, now Healing and Industry. The Strains are abandoning the manors!" a man told a woman as the girls passed.

"It can't be true. How could such a thing happen?" The woman shook her head.

"They've evacuated all the manors, though, until the cause can be discovered . . ." The conversation faded in the distance.

Zeb exhaled. "He's gotten further than I expected if three

manors are already compromised."

"At least fewer people will be hurt if he succeeds."

A crowd of fellows and aides milled about in front of Art.

Zeb touched Leilani's shoulder. "Be careful and good luck."

Leilani slipped into the throng.

"Why can't we be inside? It's cold," a young fellow on her left moaned. "The Strains are fine in Art. It could just be Research."

"Research *and* Healing *and* Industry," someone interrupted her.

Leilani eyed the guard standing on the path up to Art. How could she get past him? No wall surrounded Art, just an open courtyard filled with statues. If something distracted the guard, she could run across this and disappear inside before anyone noticed.

"Do you have any ideas?" she whispered to the Strains. They responded in a high, staccato tapping, like someone drumming on the edge of a cymbal. That probably would've meant something to Zeb, or any other Highmost. Leilani, however, was on her own.

She touched Brick's wristlet. What must it be like for him, trapped in darkness? Even as buoyant as his spirits were, he had to be terrified. She unclipped her cuff and ran to the guard.

He was perhaps twenty, burlier than Brick, and with more typical Gelian coloring, blue eyed and fair haired.

"Are you deaf?" She drew a line from her ear to her mouth, like Brick had shown her.

He nodded. She drew a deep breath and tried to remember every sign Brick had taught her. She passed him the cuff. He raised his eyebrows.

Linking her fingers and thumb together, then touching her chest, she looked him directly in the eye as she explained, "My friend is hurt." She hesitated before making a wincing face and doubling over as if in pain.

His face clouded. He swept his hand forward, palm up,

then shrugged.

She chewed her bottom lip. "Where? Oh Strains. Research. How do I say Research?"

This guard apparently lacked Brick's lip reading skill. He shook his head. She fumbled through her bag for a notepad and markstone stick. His eyes brightened when she withdrew them.

Brick's in the main hallway at Research Manor. He needs help. Someone needs to get him to Healing.

The guard read her note and rubbed his chin. With his thumb, he pointed over his shoulder towards Art, saluted, then walked his fingers up his arm.

"You need to get your captain? I can." She touched her chest, walked her fingers as he had, and pointed to Art. He grinned, tapped his fist on his chest, and took off through the crowd.

Leilani hurried into the manor. Brick would have help, and she had unquestioned access to Art. She'd done it.

The gallery took up the majority of the ground level, and the open floor plan made it easy to find the door to the tunnels. She picked the lock in record time. For a moment she wondered how Zeb would handle the Strain-proof locks. Maybe Vickers had loaned her a key. He had a pistol, after all, and she could imagine him shooting the lock open. Given the option, she would've liked to try that as well.

The Strains still danced around her, suggesting Kasan hadn't made it here yet. She needed to disable the collectors so that once he did arrive, he wouldn't be able to use them. Wishing Zeb had included a hammer or wrench with her "necessary tools," she fished a light tube from her bag and shook it.

Vickers had been right. The tunnels beneath Art appeared identical to those under Research. The whole thing gave Leilani an unnerving case of deja vu. At least this time the Strains sang to her. Their subtle melodies gave her hope.

"You know, Strains," she said, "Goodly said you are

messengers from a loving Maker. If such a being exists, I could use him right now. Muddling on by myself is all well and good, but if he sent us the Strains, he must care what happens to us. Maybe he could lend me a hand?"

Nothing miraculous happened, but the Strains grew more jubilant. Leilani could clearly hear the harmonizing melodies of multiple instruments: fiddles and flutes, drums and cymbals. She smiled.

She turned into the last corridor before the ladder. Kasan stood, back to her, only a few yards ahead. Her heart leaped into her throat, and she staggered back into the darkness. She drew a deep breath and prayed she'd imagined it, but even as she did, the shuffling of his footsteps denied her this delusion. Perhaps he hadn't seen her?

"You can come out, Miss Weaver." His voice echoed. "It's too late, either way."

She shrank back against the wall. Maybe she had bungled, but she was not about to serve herself up on a platter. She drew Brick's saber. The blade dipped and rose with her trembles.

The hum of the Strains grew airy, like an old woman gasping for her last breath.

No, don't leave. Don't leave me now! Leilani backed away from the corner, but the Strains disappeared like water running from a cracked pot.

"The collectors are already on. It is only a matter of time before the dead spot consumes the entirety of this manor, as it no doubt already has the others. Your world is ending. Let me see your hands, and I'll escort you to safety. You're as Common as they come. No need for you to get caught up in the Highmosts' mess."

She imagined drawing the Strains about her as thread, but if they were thread, they were as frail as a spider web. Every time she got a hold on them, they snapped and melted, pulled into the collectors' vortex.

Just run. Run and get help. You can't fight him without the

Strains.

She managed to push off the wall. Her feet pounded down the hallway, echoing loudly. Something whooshed by her ear, and she skidded to a stop. The Strain-grenade impacted against the floor several yards in front of her. She yelped and covered her ears and eyes.

The wave rushed over her. Without the protection of Brick's bracer, the shockwave hit her chest like a sledge hammer. She crumpled to her hands and knees. Her light tube clattered to the floor and rolled towards Kasan. The former aide crushed it under his foot. Luminescent liquid seeped out, to puddle on the floor.

He swung his lantern over Leilani. Her ears rang. She could see but as if through a fishbowl, and the Strains . . . the Strains were gone.

She grit her teeth. He stepped closer. Air slowly made its way back into her lungs. She clenched her fingers around the saber.

"I wonder how you survived the first one I tossed at you. Well, this one didn't miss." Kasan kicked her in the side.

She struck out, whipping the blade towards him.

Kasan yelped as the saber sank into his calf. He yanked his leg backwards. Blood mingled with the glowing puddle, and a sickening smell filled the air.

"You little drudge! I should've known you wouldn't understand." He reached into a pocket and produced another grenade.

With all her might, Leilani lurched to her feet and barreled into his stomach. Kasan fell backwards. Momentum pushed Leilani on, and she tumbled around the corner. Kasan came after her, clutching the grenade above his head. She gained her footing and sprinted to the end of the corridor. As the second grenade exploded overhead, she dropped down the hole into the market room. She scrambled into the darkness.

Flecks of dirt rained down on her head, and she

remembered what Vickers had said about the tunnels being structurally unsound. She shuddered and hid behind the nearest column.

The light from Kasan's lantern announced his descent into the room. The hissing of the collector's valves beat out an unnerving rhythm. Hiss, clank, hiss. She needed to disable those machines, but with what? It wasn't as if she had pockets full of Strains-powered-death-dealing-missiles to toss.

An idea popped into her head like a book falling open to the right page. She dodged from one column to the next, putting herself a little closer to the middle of the room. She continued in her column hugging path. The light from his lantern caused the shadows to bend first one way, then another, around her. She managed to always keep a pillar of stone between herself and Kasan.

"You know this is futile." His voice floated about, mingling with the workings of the collectors and the silence left by the Strains. "It's too late. The first of the manors should've crumbled by now."

She slipped through the shadows to a new hiding spot. A blast rocked an area several columns away. Grit rained from the ceiling, and she ducked.

"I have plenty left. Want to keep playing this game?"

Leilani counted the columns to the center of the room: three more jumps should do it. She drew a deep breath and tightened her hold about the saber's hilt.

"The shameful thing is, you aren't even one of them," Kasan continued. "You're just a favored pet, like my brother. You know where that got him. You'll never belong with the Highmost, little Common girl."

An argument that would've been more convincing before you tried to blow me up.

She slipped to the next column.

He gave a cry of triumph.

Realizing she'd been seen, she sprinted out of the way

even as a grenade slammed into her former hiding place. The stone cracked, and the column sagged.

Leilani's chin collided with the dirt floor, and her teeth sank into her tongue. Blood tainted her mouth. The saber clattered away from her. She struggled forward on her hands and knees. Kasan stepped into the gap between the next two pillars and grinned down at her, his foot on top of her blade.

With one hand on the nearest column for support, she stood.

He tossed a grenade up and down. "Actually, I lied about plenty. This is my last one, but it should be sufficient." He pulled back his arm.

Everything seemed to slow down. She watched the arch of the weapon as it hurtled towards her. Instinctively, she put her hand up. It smacked against her fingers, and with one fluid motion and all her might, she hurled it towards the collectors.

Kasan shrieked. "No!" He dove after it.

The grenade collided against the collectors and detonated. The Strains' death wail expanded, thrusting Kasan back like a leaf caught in a windstorm. The columns nearest the explosion cracked.

Leilani dashed for the ladder. Debris rained down on her head. She glanced back. Strains whistled through a hole in the side of one of the collectors. The other three, however, appeared uncompromised.

Kasan's grenades had already weakened the room. If she didn't stop the collectors, Art could collapse.

Ignoring the shrill cries of the Strains and Kasan's crumpled body, she sprinted to the middle of the room. She flipped valves open, and the joyous cries of liberated Strains mingled with the agonized shouts of the dying.

"This is over," she snarled. "No one will do this to you again." Two collectors disabled, she stepped over Kasan's body to the third.

A grinding sound caused her to turn. A column slipped to

the side, toppling like a tree, towards her. She darted out of the way. The heavy stones crushed the last collector like a tin can. Strains burst from it, and the room shook. She fought through the crumbling rocks and choking dust. Kasan's lantern blinked out as she reached the foot of the ladder. The metal rungs vibrated beneath her fingers. Leilani made it up two steps before her hands slipped. She fell back onto the ground.

Lights danced before her, spots of brightness against the sheet of black. The stars faded and all was silent and cold.

Chapter Twenty-Six

Leilani woke to a throbbing headache and the smell of clean cotton. She inhaled and let the breath chase the aches from the corners of her mind. The Strains droned a lullaby, like a harmony of buzzing bees. Slowly, she opened her eyes.

An oil lamp flickered on the table beside her. Her forehead felt stiff. Raising her hand to her brow, she found it bandaged. Her clothes had been replaced by a white night shirt.

A few feet away, three people stood beside another bed, their backs to her. She recognized Zeb's lopsided braid and Vickers's stature. The man to Vickers's left was nearly as tall as Vickers but with gray streaked hair.

"You are right, Miss Brightly," the older man said. "Carefully controlled exposure to amplified Strains might reverse the damage. I believe that was the cure when Fellow Verge's assistant fell victim to Strains blindness. The question is, at what frequency?"

"I'm sure the healers at the time left records," Vickers said with a snort. "It isn't as if we have to repeat their research, just replicate the results."

The older man turned his head enough for Leilani to see his scowl. Vickers turned his back to him, and the movement allowed Leilani to see Brick, sleeping in the bed. He looked so peaceful that she almost hushed the Highmost, before realizing it didn't matter.

The older man cleared his throat. "I'll check the record room. Will you come with me, Vickers? The work will be quicker with two."

Vickers shifted from foot to foot but nodded and followed the man out.

Zeb glanced over her shoulder, and her eyes lit up. "Leilani, oh thank the Strains!" She scraped a chair across the room and sat at Leilani's bedside.

"Is this Healing?" Leilani asked as she sat up in bed.

"Yes. They found you hours ago, after Vickers explained what was going on to the guards at Civics and we realized you were missing. The market room under Art is covered in rubble, but thankfully we found you on top of it, not under it. It looked as if you almost made it out. Did you see Kasan?"

Leilani grimaced. "He was in the market room too. It might take a while to dig him up, however."

Zeb shuddered. "So much dying, though after what he did . . . Anyway, I had them move you in here because I thought you'd want to see Brick when you came to."

Leilani smiled. "Thank you. It sounds as if there is hope?"

"Oh, yes. That man is Vickers's father. They kind of have a difficult relationship, but he's brilliant, so Vickers asked him to help. It took a lot of pride swallowing on Vickers's part. I thanked him for you, a couple of times." Zeb grinned, then blushed, then twisted her braid. "Anyway, he thinks we can fix Brick."

Relief flooded Leilani's chest, and she exhaled. She swung her legs out of bed.

Zeb picked Leilani's bag off the floor. "Here. I'll leave so you can change. I want to see if Vickers needs my help. Also, I know they sent for Brick's mother. You might want some time alone with him before she shows up. I know I would, anyway."

Zeb left, and Leilani turned the chair to face Brick's bed. She dug out a change of clothes, pulling on a pair of leggings and replacing the nightshirt with a knee length smock. Even though he was asleep, and temporarily unable to see her even if awake, she still flushed and averted her eyes from him as she changed. She settled into the chair when finished.

His hand rested outside the blankets. She slipped her fingers into it. He started awake, so she tightened her grip and brought his palm to her face.

His thumb stroked her chin, and a weak smiled played across his lips. With his free hand, he circled his face, signing *beautiful* again.

"I wish I could be as brave as you," she whispered. "I'd face a thousand grenades before enduring what you're going through right now."

The door behind her creaked open. Flory entered the room, her brows furrowed together. Her eyes glistened. Seeing Leilani, she gave a haggard smile.

Leilani started to rise, but Flory put her hand out.

"Please. I know you're comforting him. The nurse in the hallway remembered me from my manor days. She told me what happened and that the prognosis is good." She stepped around Leilani's chair and ruffled her son's hair. He grabbed her wrist and followed it up to her face. He made a rocking motion with his arm and stroked his cheek. She laughed, pulled his hand to her face, and nodded. Flory and Leilani sat in silence, watching over Brick. Eventually he fell asleep once more.

Leilani related the story of their adventures as he slept. She had just gotten to where Zeb attacked the door with the broken hammer when Vickers entered the room.

"My father will be back in a moment. He and Zeb went to get the original amplifier from stor. . ." Vickers's voice died in his throat. His hands fell limp at his side, and his lower jaw went slack.

Flory staggered to her feet, drawing a jagged breath.

"Mom?" Vickers voice was almost a whimper. His usually stoic presence melted, and for a moment, his face resembled a lost child's.

Flory stumbled forward and touched his arm. "Vick? Is it really you? Oh look at you. You're so tall."

Leilani's mind raced. *Vickers and Flory? Then Vickers and Brick? Oh Strains. Does Brick know?*

She stepped back, pressing herself into the wall to avoid coming between them, but it probably wouldn't matter. They didn't even look in her direction.

Flory embraced Vickers. He held back, his eyes squeezed shut.

After a moment he withdrew and glanced at Brick. "He's your son?"

She nodded. "I married his father shortly after you were taken from me. I wanted to tell you about him, but I was afraid you'd beg to meet him. It is hard enough getting one little boy to keep a secret, let alone two, though neither of you are boys any more."

"I'm sorry he was hurt. He's getting the best care possible, though. My father . . . oh Strains, this is going to be awkward."

"I am not afraid of your father," Flory said. "If he's willing to help Brick, I'm grateful. What happened between us was a long time ago. He doesn't know that you know me, does he?"

Vickers shook his head.

"Good. We can keep it that way. It will make it easier for us to see each other in the future." She touched her son's cheek. "You are everything I dreamed for you. I am so thankful to see you again."

Leilani cleared her throat. "I'll step outside if you two want to talk for a while."

"Thank you," Vickers said, opening the door for her.

Outside of the small sick room was an open hall with skylights, benches, and many more doors, presumably leading to more small sick rooms. She sat upon a bench, her head spinning. Brick and Vickers were brothers? Half-brothers, but brothers still. When Zebedy heard that, her head would likely explode. Well, that was for Vickers to tell her.

Zeb and Mr. Buffet came down the hall. A man in a white apron wheeled a cart with the amplifier on it after them. The men and the amplifier entered the sick room, but Zeb settled next to Leilani.

"We'll know in a few minutes if it works or not," she said. "The Strains think it will. They've been cheering me on this whole time. Loudly. Even Fellow Buffet, Vickers's father, could hear them. He thinks I should switch manors to Healing."

Leilani raised her eyebrows. "Do you want to?"

"I don't know. I don't necessarily want to return to Research, not with all that has happened. Too many ghosts." Zeb rubbed her hands on her knees. "I don't know if working here would be good for me and Vickers . . . me and Vickers. It feels so weird saying that." Her laugh fluttered and the Strains vibrated along, like fingers gliding over a harp.

Leilani patted her friend's shoulder. "For what it is worth, I think Vickers is the kind who will stay with you no matter what you choose. He's a good man, steady. You could use some steady."

"You've always been my steady." Zeb smiled.

"And I always will be, but Vickers is good for you, too."

"Yes. I kind of always knew he was. I just thought he didn't like me. It's weird how wrong I can be about people when I know so much about the Strains. I was right about you, though." The two girls embraced.

The door opened, and Vickers stepped out. "Leilani, you might want to see this."

Hand in hand, Zeb and Leilani followed Vickers back into the room. Mr. Buffet had attached two black suction cups, one over each of Brick's eyes. Both led to the amplifier through snakey tubes. He adjusted the dials on the amplifier, and a high but sweet note hummed through the room.

"It may only be a partial restoration at first," he said. "We'll probably need to schedule multiple treatments over the next week, though we should be able to tell immediately if it is working or not."

Leilani knelt at Brick's bedside. Buffet peeled off the cups, and Brick stared wide eyed at the ceiling. He blinked. His pupils darted from side to side before his gaze fell upon Leilani.

She smiled.

Tears welled in his eyes. He bolted up and pulled her to his chest. Squeezed against him, she let herself cry. The Strains laughed about her, melding with the happy cries of Flory and Zeb. Brick kissed the top of Leilani's head. She raised her face to his.

Their lips met. The Strains began a symphony, and Leilani's heart sang along with them.

Chapter Twenty-Seven

Leilani and Brick walked hand and hand up to Art Manor. A cold breeze whistled about them, and she shivered, wishing she hadn't let the bright spring sun fool her into not wearing a cloak. Brick grinned, a spring in his step in spite of the chill.

The Strains swirled around them, fluttering like bird's wings.

They reached the steps. Brick glanced at the door then back at Leilani. He let go of her hand so he could sign.

She watched his fingers closely then looked up at his eyes to reply. "I know I can't follow you into class, but I wanted to see you here. It's your first day. That's a big deal."

He ran his fingertips down the side of her face. He stepped up one step, turned back, smiled, and signed some more.

"Dinner, tonight," she agreed. She tapped her lips with her fingers then touched her fingers to the back of her hand, hoping she got the gestures right this time. He didn't chuckle, so she must've been close. "It's a date."

She watched him disappear into the building. Other manor students, some wearing brown and gray Common clothes, passed her. She hadn't realized how many Common folk attended Art until Brick received his overdue scholarship. It was swiftly becoming Leilani's favorite manor.

"Leilani!"

She turned at the voice. Zeb waved as she ran up. "I thought I'd find you here. Vick told me Brick started today."

Leilani rolled her eyes. "Vick? Is that what you're calling him now? Seriously, that will get confusing."

Zeb shrugged. "I call him Vicky in private, but he asked me to avoid it around others . . . I guess you're probably excluded from others. Anyway, he won't mind."

"Well, I'll stick with Vickers rather than Vicky. I owe him that. If he wasn't helping Flory, Brick would still be a guard rather than finally attending Art."

Zeb grinned. "I knew we'd marry brothers, and I *did* get the older one . . ."

Leilani held up her hand. "No one is getting married yet. Strains, you're worse than Keris."

A breath of wind pushed a strand of Zeb's hair in her face. She brushed it back. "Come on, there's something we need to talk about, but I told Vickers I'd meet him at Civics . . . let's walk and talk."

With no manor posting, Zeb had moved back in with her parents who were trying unsuccessfully to get her to join the "less dangerous" Weather Manor.

Unwilling to step backwards, Leilani had opted to stay with Keris and Jess, occasionally helping out with Jess's carpentry jobs. Keris respected Leilani's privacy for the most part, not mentioning her failed stint with the Highmost. She did, however, tease about wanting to see her little sister settled into her own happy marriage. Leilani managed to slip away to the Manor District most days, to spend time with Brick and Zeb.

They stepped out into the street. Zeb cleared her throat. "So, I've been bouncing around the manors, looking for a good fit, but nothing has seemed quite right. Then a couple of weeks ago, Vickers told me about Brick's Art appointment, and it got me wondering, why is Art the only manor to accept Common applicants? I mean, some Common work in Healing, Civics, and Industry, but they are all in menial positions. None of them get a chance at fellowships.

"They say it's because Common folk can't handle the various tasks required by the manors, but I think you've proven, to me anyway, that's just ridiculous. So I started writing– apparently I'm good at writing. It's like talking, a little slower, but basically talking.

"Anyway, I started writing this paper about all the various

tasks done by the manors and how they could be accomplished by Common as well as Highmost, and when I was done, I gave it to Vickers, just to see what he thought, and he gave it to the Highmost of Civics. . ." Zeb stopped and glanced at Leilani.

Leilani nodded. "And then?"

The Strains began a quick paced melody of pipes and drums.

Zeb held up her hands. "I'm getting there! Strains, the Strains can be impatient sometimes." She shrugged and started walking again. "Anyway, Highmost Patent asked me for a meeting, and then another meeting, and another. She likes the way I express ideas. Also, she was impressed by how you helped with the collector crisis. Your part in it hasn't been as openly talked about, so she didn't know until I told her. She asked me to put together a plan to integrate a scholarship program for Common across all six manors."

Leilani's mouth dropped, and her feet froze to the cobblestones.

"Hey, out of the way!" a merchant in a horse-drawn cart shouted, and both girls scurried from the street into the courtyard of Civics Manor.

"It needs to be approved by the Highmost Seat–"

"But you're dating the Highmost Seat's son," Leilani interrupted.

Zeb blushed. "Yes. Vick thinks his father will say yes, if I can iron out any budgetary issues and think up an application process that makes sense."

The girls climbed the marble steps into the lobby. Clerks and junior fellows rushed about with stacks of papers, none giving the pair a second glance. Zeb and Leilani entered the poorly lit back halls that led to Vickers's office.

"This all sounds wonderful. Can you do it? The budgetary and application issues?" Leilani asked.

Zeb grimaced. "Apparently I am much better at 'expressing ideas' than I am about figuring out a ledger. I've never dealt with a budget in my life. Vickers has helped me a bit, but he has his own projects, and I can't depend on him to do everything for me . . . Anyway, that's what he said when it led to our first 'couple fight.' We kissed and made up, but the snapping at each other over balance sheets wasn't fun."

Leilani snorted. "Yeah, I imagine not. That's the only benefit to me being so poor at signing. It's hard to fight if you have to think so carefully about every word before you sign it."

Zeb grabbed Leilani's hand. "I want you to help me."

Leilani raised her eyebrows. "No!" she said firmly. "We have been down this path. I am *not* going to be your aide again. Not now, not ever–"

The Strains blared a high pitched tone, and Leilani winced.

"They say, 'listen.'" Zeb squeezed Leilani's fingers. "That's not what I meant. You're just as smart as me and probably twice as competent. Honestly, if either of us could do this alone, it's you, but there needs to be at least one Highmost involved for them to take the project seriously. I'm not saying it is right, but that's the way it is, and we need to work with that for the time being."

Leilani's brows furrowed. "What are you saying, then?"

"It's a partnership. We are going to work *together*. If you are willing that is." Zeb's eyes grew wide and earnest.

Leilani hesitated.

This is going to be a lot of work. Two steps forward, one step back sort of work, probably, and working with Zeb might actually be fun if she isn't able to tell me what to do.

Zeb gripped Leilani's wrist harder. "Please, Leilani, I need you, but it isn't just that. All of Gelia needs you."

Leilani smiled. "No, Zeb. It needs *us*."

The End

ABOUT H. L. BURKE

Born in a small town in north central Oregon, H. L. Burke spent most of her childhood around trees and farm animals and always accompanied by a book. Growing up with epic heroes from Middle Earth and Narnia keeping her company, she also became an incurable romantic.

An addictive personality, she jumped from one fandom to another, being at times completely obsessed with various books, movies, or television series (Lord of the Rings, Star Wars, and Star Trek all took their turns), but she has grown to be what she considers a well-rounded connoisseur of geek culture.

Married to her high school crush who is now a US Marine, she has moved multiple times in her adult life but believes home is wherever her husband, two daughters, and pets are.

For information about H. L. Burke's latest novels, author news and events, or to contact the writer, go to
www.hlburkeauthor.com

Made in the USA
San Bernardino, CA
27 May 2018